MY FIRST LOVE
&
OTHER DISASTERS

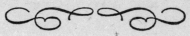

FRANCINE PASCAL

LAUREL-LEAF BOOKS bring together under a single imprint out-standing works of fiction and nonfiction particularly suitable for young adult readers, both in and out of the classroom. Charles F. Reasoner, Professor Emeritus of Children's Literature and Reading, New York University, is consultant to this series.

Published by
Dell Publishing Co., Inc.
1 Dag Hammarskjold Plaza
New York, New York 10017

To my parents
Kate and William Rubin

Laurel-Leaf Library ® TM 766734, Dell Publishing Co., Inc.

YOUNG LOVE® is a trademark of DC COMICS INC.

ISBN: 0-440-95447-9

RL: 4.9

Reprinted by arrangement with The Viking Press
Viking Penguin, Inc.
Printed in the United States of America
First Laurel-Leaf printing—April 1980
Seventh Laurel-Leaf printing—August 1982

1

When I think about all the time I wasted last year moaning about how gross it was to be thirteen, I could kick myself. Thirteen turned out to be fantastic. It had to be. I mean, you finally make it. You're in the graduating class, and even if it's only the top of a bunch of little kids, it still makes you feel really special. Yes, sir, thirteen was definitely first-rate. But fourteen? Forget it. It's the pits.

There are so many horrendous things about being fourteen that I'd freak out if I had to name half of them. Just think about it. One day you're the biggest big shot in the entire elementary school (among the girls anyway) and the next you're little Miss Nobody, which is exactly what everyone else in the whole high school seems to think about freshmen. At least that's the way they treat us.

Another bummer is how long it takes. Growing up, I mean. Except for times like Christmas vacation and summer, it seems like the years take forever to drag by. And for the plans I'm making I absolutely have to be fifteen practically instantly. Especially seeing as how the person I happen to be madly in love with is seventeen and the person he's absolutely crazy about is sixteen. I'm definitely nowhere, sitting around being only fourteen, but it's absolutely hopeless—I mean, there's nothing I can do about it until I'm fifteen. Oh, sure, I'm getting there. But it's going to take me two more enormous weeks. I don't know how I'm going to stand the wait.

I probably forgot to tell you that there's another small problem aside from Miss Sweet Sixteen, and that is that the love of my life has absolutely no idea that I even exist. But no sweat. I've arranged for our beautiful meeting to take place Tuesday at Howell's. I guess a shoe store for the orthopedically fashionable doesn't sound like the most romantic place for an encounter, but that's where he works on weekdays after school. They only other choice was his Saturday job—digging cesspools. Anyway, I'm not worried, because I've worked out every single detail, so it can't miss. Theoretically. Of course in the real world, the one where practically everything I touch bites me, not only can it miss but it'll probably boomerang and come right back and hit me in the face.

No doubt it'll fail in some simple way, like I'll trip on my shoelaces. Big deal, so what if I'm not wearing shoelaces. I can always trip on somebody else's.

Or worse yet, I'll do what I did when my class went backstage at *I Love My Wife* last year and we met the whole cast. I was so nervous and excited I thought I'd faint. Somebody said, "Victoria, I'd like you to meet Tommy Smothers—this is Victoria Martin." I smiled and said as sweetly as possible, "Hello, Victoria." And everybody broke up.

Or what if it's something even more horrible? Suppose I'm standing there meeting the love of my life, and I'm smiling, and I don't know it but I have this black smudge across my nose, or worse, a crumb is stuck to my lip. Everything would be absolutely ruined. You know how it is when something like that happens, you can't even hear what the person is saying—all you do is stare at the crumb. But I think I may have that one beat because I'm bringing my best friend with me and she's going to be my crumb spotter, which will work perfectly unless she starts laughing. We both do that at the most embarrassing times—break up, I mean. But she's much worse than I am.

Anyway, about that dream guy of mine, after we get past that first meeting and we come to know each other, then I get right to work dumping the competition. But I don't do that here, in New York City—I do it on Fire Island. That's this super fabulous beach resort on Long Island where absolutely all the action is in the summertime. Anyway, *he's* going to be there for the whole summer and *she* isn't.

The first part is ready to move, but the Fire Island stuff could be sticky. I've got to get my parents' permission to be a mother's helper for the summer. For my parents that's the equivalent of asking them to let me hitchhike through Tasmania with the janitor. Still, I'm not discouraged because I know that the first time you try to get permission for anything new from your parents it always looks impossible, but if you keep at them long enough (and I've been at it all month long) they finally wear down.

So let's just say that I do get to meet him and somehow I convince my parents to allow me to go to Fire Island, then there's one more little side thing that I have to take care of.

There's this other boy, Barry. He's a complication. You see, I don't really know him, but he likes me. Which sounds peculiar, but it's one of those things where you can tell somebody's got a crush on you because they always turn up wherever you go, and you catch them staring at you all the time, and crazy things like that. Anyway, I have to get friendly with him because it just so happens that he's a friend of Jim's, and he has a house on Fire Island, and I understand that Jim hangs out there a lot. I haven't figured out how to handle getting to be Barry's just-plain-friend-not-girl-friend yet. But I will.

Anyway, the first thing I have to pull off is the big meeting this Tuesday.

Now that you got that all straight, let me tell you a little more about the most important part—Jimmy.

2

The first time I saw Jimmy I thought, what is every-body making such a fuss about? I mean, so okay, he's gorgeous looking, so what's the big deal about that, and why is practically every single freshperson (I'm getting very heavy into women's lib lately) at Cooper High bug-eyed about him?

Actually, I figured that with all those girls dropping at his feet he had to be the most conceited, egocentric, me-me-me-type goon around. The kind I stay far away from.

Well, that was nearly ten months ago, and it's in-credible but I think he gets better looking every day. All I have to do is catch a quick peek at him in the hall or even from halfway across the gym and I'm posi-tively knocked out. I don't know, maybe it has some-thing to do with that number he does to keep his gor-geous straight silky blond hair from falling into his sexy hazel green-brown eyes. He kind of dips his head down and to the side a little and then flips it back. Two seconds later the gorgeous blond hair slides back down over his eyes again. I could watch him do that forever. In fact, one time I was doing just that when he looked up and caught me, and I had to pretend I was looking for someone in the row behind him. It didn't work so well because unfortunately, at the time, he was sitting in the last row.

Did I tell you that he's about six feet tall and he's got the most sensational body I've ever seen in my entire life? It's not all that different from everyone else's —I mean, it's got the same number of things—but on him it all seems to fit so perfectly.

I probably sound like I'm very superficial and that all I'm interested in is his looks. That's not true, because I know there's a lot more to Jim than just his looks. For one thing, he's the kind of person everybody always wants to hang out with. And not just girls. Guys too. Maybe that's because he always looks like he's having such a good time. I suppose it's his smile. It's the catching kind. Makes you feel up just to look at him.

He's been the president of his class for two years running, and the captain of the tennis team, so obviously I'm not the only one who thinks he's terrific.

One tiny little thing. He *probably* knows he's something special, but he'd have to be blind or a hypocrite not to. Actually he just looks like he feels good about himself, and I don't think that's so bad.

Obviously, I've completely freaked out over him. And like I said, he doesn't know I'm alive. But that's okay because Steffi (the friend I told you about) and I have decided that the situation is pretty viable (my mother's favorite word; no matter what you talk to her about, you've got to figure that somehow something in it is going to be "viable." It got so bad I finally had to look it up).

Anyway, it's still definitely viable except for that one disgusting, ugly, grungy problem. Her name is Gloria, and she's been his girl friend since the start of his junior year, which makes it almost a year that she's been going more or less steady with him. And that's not even the worst. Steffi and I did a little digging and we came up with a lot more bad news. Number one is that she's his sister's best friend. Number two, she lives in his apartment building. And number three is the real killer—she's sixteen. I would sell my kid sister's soul (and all the rest of her too) to be sixteen. But what's the use. Nobody's buying.

Even Steffi admits Gloria shoots a big hole in the viability angle. Especially when you see her and Jimmy together. She's always right there, hanging on to his arm like she was drowning. She'd better cool it or he's going to wake up one morning with one six-foot-long arm. I hate to think what his sweaters must look like. And she's a whiner—"Jim . . . my, I'm hungry—Jim . . . my, I'm thirsty—Jim . . . my, I'm cold—Jim . . . my, you promised. . . ." She's not as bad as my sister, Nina, but for a practically adult person she's pretty awful. And on top of that she's also one of those really girlish types of squeamish, too-too precious, dainty things that'd faint dead away if they saw one measly little worm. You know, the kind that's always wearing some guy's jacket or sweater because she's shivering, even in August. Very dependent type. You don't see too many of them around anymore since women's lib. She's the last of a dying breed, and we should probably preserve her. In fact that would be a perfect solution. Have her stuffed.

Her and Norman. Norman's my sheepdog, and even though it's horrendous to talk that way about your own dog, with Norman it would probably be a month before anyone noticed the difference. It seems like all he ever does is sleep or watch Nina—that's my twelve-year-old sister—and me argue about whose turn it is to take him out.

We've had Norman forever, and for a long time we thought he had some kind of psychological block against showing affection, but now we realize that the only reason he doesn't give us those big leaping doggy greetings with all the kissing and tailwagging is simply because it takes too much energy. If he could figure a way to do it without getting up I know he would, because deep down he really loves us—except for that thing he has about us plotting to steal his food. My father says he's paranoid, but I don't think he's any worse than Nina when it comes to something she loves. First thing she does is spit on it. (That definitely discourages sharing.) She's a real winner anyway. It seems like she's always hanging around, butting in, bugging my friends, tattling, whining, borrowing and never returning, and generally being a pain in the neck. She also looks like a troll—well, to me anyway, although she has nice greenish eyes if you can find them under her glasses. And they say she'll have pretty teeth when the railroad tracks come off. (I'm wired, too, but not with tracks—the thin kind that's almost invisible.)

Listen, I know Typhoid Mary was worse, but she wasn't my sister. My mother keeps assuring me that it's natural for siblings to think they hate each other as kids but that there's really a deep well of love (her words) that we'll discover when we're older. She's probably right—when I'm about a hundred I should start liking Nina.

Actually, in this last year she's made two big improvements. One is her hair. It used to hang in strings like grunge. Then she made a brilliant discovery—shampoo. The second thing is her trick belch. You know what it's like to introduce some great guy to your sister and instead of "hello" she takes a monster breath and . . . well, that's the second improvement. Now she only does it around the house with family and close friends. She's still got a long way to go.

I probably ought to count my blessings. Steffi's brother still picks his nose and he's nearly fourteen.

Say I eventually do get Nina under control. That still leaves the real tough ones, Felicia and Philip Martin, terrific, fabulous, sensational people except when it comes to being my parents. The problem is so obvious to me. They take their job too seriously. I'm two seconds away from being fifteen, and they're still hanging over me, making sure I eat a proper breakfast, wear my scarf, my boots, my gloves, my sweater, and then there are all those watch-outs—watch the knife, your fingers, the bottom step, the car door, sharp corners, strangers, drafts, and fishbones. To be absolutely fair, I think they've gotten it together a lot this past year. Four different times in the last month neither of them warned me that I was going to tip over and crack my head when I leaned back on the dining-room chairs.

I guess it's always possible that they've just stopped caring about my head, but I don't really think so. I'm an optimist and I think they were just going through a bad stage and now they're improving. Like now, they're actually considering the possibility of me being a mother's helper this summer out on Fire Island. I definitely know my mother's considering letting me take the job, because the last time we discussed it (actually it was the seventeenth time since April) she said, "We'll see." I know from way back that "We'll see" usually stinks, but I read it as a giant step up from "Are you out of your mind?" and "Absolutely not!" For my mother, even just considering the possibility is a huge improvement.

Naturally she still hassles me to do things her way, but now she's starting to listen to my side a lot more and even tries to let me make more decisions on my own. Even so, she has a long way to go—a lot further than my father, who's pretty okay except when it comes to boys. It's like he thinks they're all out to steal his precious baby. When it comes to his darling daughters, he's just like Norman with his food. You should see the looks he gives them—the boys, I mean. Nickie Rostivo says it feels like my father's looking right through him. And Dad's definitely outrageous when it comes to any boy I show just the teensiest romantic interest in. Still, mostly he's pretty fabulous.

Anyway, back to sensational Jimmy. I think I'll start calling him Jim just to be different. I'm only just starting, so if I want him to notice me I've got to be special, which is a horrendous problem when you are as ordinary average as me. I'm sure just calling him Jim isn't going to make him stop dead and say, "Who is that mysterious average-looking girl who is courageous enough to call me Jim when the rest of the world still calls me Jimmy?" Still, it's a start, and I need all the starts I can get.

Naturally I've been doing some dumb things like calling him on the phone and giggling. It's okay because I never say my name. I'd die if he ever found out.

Anyway, like I said, Steffi and I have a plan of attack that's really far out. We're going to go into the store where Jim works part time and pretend I need a pair of shoes. You should see the shoes. They're great looking if you happen to have hoofs. Luckily, I've saved enough baby-sitting money so I could buy a cheap pair if I absolutely had to. I don't expect him to fall over dead at the sight of me, but at least I'll get to meet him.

I've created the scene in my mind a hundred times, and it always comes out beautiful. I go in there and there's nobody around but him, and he comes out and it's one of those things like in the movies, where his eyes and my eyes meet and we stand there held to each other while the electricity crackles around us. Then finally he pulls himself away and I sit down (I'm wearing my new John Kloss nightgown) and he starts to take off my shoes and the touch of his hand on my bare foot stuns us both. (In dreams you don't have to wear peds to try on shoes.) So then he asks me what shoes I want and I tell him and he can't stop looking at me. Then there's a whole boring part where he brings out the shoes and tries them on me and that whole thing, and then finally when I'm about to leave (in this one I get stuck buying a really horrendous pair of espadrilles, but I figure I can always sell them to

Nina), he says he has to see me, and he's shocked when I tell him that I go to school with him, and we plan to go out that Saturday night, and I can tell he's got to break a date with Gloria. Anyway, that's the dream.

Today is real life, and it's that Tuesday afternoon I told you about, and I'm waiting for Steffi to buzz me from the lobby, and then we're going over to Howell's shoe store because this is the day that Jim works there.

My complexion looks sort of okay today. There are a lot of under-the-skin bumps that nobody else ever seems to see, but I do. Still, if nobody else can, I guess he won't, so it doesn't matter. I'm wearing Steffi's new French jeans, my cousin Liz's suede clogs (we traded, I gave her my old Adidas sneakers, which always killed my little toe anyway), and this fabulous Indian shirt I gave my mother for her last birthday.

My hair is only so-so because I didn't have time to wash it, and it's been almost two days since my last shampoo so it's really disgusting. I washed my feet anyway.

It must be three-thirty because jerk-face just got home. That's Nina.

"You walk Norman!" I tell her first thing.

"Is Mommy home?" she answers.

"Walk him now!"

"Is Mommy home!" she keeps insisting.

"No."

"Up yours, shithead, I'll walk him when I feel like it." She's a monster when my mother is out. If my mother ever heard the language her darling twelve-year-old uses, she'd have a conniption. I'm starting to tell her a few things when the downstairs buzzer rings. That has to be Steffi. I do a last-mirror check, grab my father's velour jacket that fits me perfectly since my mother accidentally put it in the dryer, and race out.

Steffi is waiting in the front of the building. For

some strange reason she's wearing her new jeans jumpsuit that she said she was saving for Myrl Weingard's birthday party next week. She's really got a fabulous figure. A lot of people can't wear jumpsuits, but she looks smashing in them. She even combed her hair a little different. I have to tell her how terrific it looks with a side part. And, my God, she's wearing eye shadow! And now that I come closer, at least half a bottle of my tea-rose perfume that I left at her house last week.

Right at this second my feelings toward my very best friend in the whole world are very confused. I'm absolutely torn between hate and loathing. I can't believe Steffi would try to steal my boyfriend even before he's really my boyfriend. I'm probably leaping to conclusions and I really should be ashamed of myself. Steffi Klinger has been my dearest friend since we met in fifth grade. (It was really hysterical how we were both crazy about this jerky guy. . . .)

Oh, damn! How could she! Well, I'm certainly not about to blow my cool over a little competition. I've always heard that competition is healthy—for potato-sack racing. Not boys. I smile sweetly at her and decide to play it tricky. "Listen," I say to her, "if you're too busy to come with me today I can do it alone or we can make it for another day."

"That's okay," she says brightly. "I can come today."

"Or better yet, I can meet you later."

"Anything you like."

"Or you could wait outside."

"Sure thing."

"You mean you don't mind not coming?"

"I swear it's okay with me. Actually, then I can go home and change. I feel so jerky all dressed up like this, but my mother wanted to take some pictures for some special album she's doing and then I didn't have time to change. I'll probably get it all grimied up, and I wanted to save it for Myrl's party."

Suddenly I love her again.

"Don't change," I say.

"You don't think it looks gross in the middle of the afternoon? And I'm wearing eye makeup too."

"You look beautiful."

"Really?"

"Absolutely."

"By the way, I owe you a new tea-rose. I spilled the whole bottle on my foor. Gross, huh?"

Did I mention that Steffi's the greatest friend in the world?

"You'll really freak them out in the shoe store," I say.

"I thought you wanted me to wait outside."

"Not a chance. I'd die if I had to go through it alone. You just have to be there."

"Super. I've been looking forward to this all day. I just know he's going to freak out when he meets you."

"You think so?"

"I know it. You look absolutely spectacular today."

"Quick. Let's go before I start to fade."

So we start to walk toward Broadway. Howell's is only about three blocks from my house. We're not even walking fast, but I'm starting to sweat just from excitement. Luckily this blouse isn't clingy so you can't see that I'm dripping wet. Damn Secret.

Oh, God, I just remembered I'm going to get my period practically any minute! Now even my face is sweaty. Well, maybe the store will be air conditioned and then I can sort of hang out near the front windows until I dry off. Unless of course I really do get my period, and then standing with my back to him would be a mistake.

Mostly when people think of Broadway they think it's all theaters and hookers, but around my way, up in the Fifties, it's really okay. And when you go farther uptown it gets great. At least I love it. You find all kinds of stores—great little clothes shops and markets—and it's always busy and noisy with a million things happening. And the people are outrageous. Not scary outrageous, just crazy and exciting. My father says there are more nuts per square inch on Broadway than on any other street in the world. Like the Lysol lady. She's some kook who runs around with a mask over her nose and mouth spraying Lysol all around her. Nothing else nutty about her. I mean she wouldn't bother anyone. She just likes things clean.

Anyway, in no time at all we're outside Howell's, and Steffi pokes me to look in the window. There he is. My Jim. He *is* gorgeous.

"Wait!" I grab Steffi just as she's about to open the door. "Let's say again what we're going to do."

"Relax," she purrs, "it's easy. All we do is go in and sit down, and when Jimmy sees you he'll come over, and from there on it's practically a snap. I mean, one look at those jeans and he'll be off the wall."

"You're the best friend I ever had, but what if he doesn't fall over dead for me?"

"He has to. I just feel it. I mean, the vibes are perfect."

"Should I have a shoe number to give him?"

"Definitely."

"Ugh. They're all so ugly. Maybe those espadrilles aren't too disgusting."

"Okay, just remember seven-oh-three."

"I got it."

"So come on. Let's go."

"Wait a sec."

"What now?"

"Maybe I should get the sneakers. At least they're not completely gross."

"Ugh, no. Sneakers are so unsexy. Stick with the espadrilles. At least they make you look taller, and he's probably six foot. Come on. They're beginning to look funny at us."

"No, wait. . . ."

"Whaa . . . t!"

"I forgot the number."

"Seven-oh-three. Now let's go." And she opens the door and shoves me in. Oh, God!

We're in the store and it's a lot smaller than I thought. There's no room to just stand there and dry off. There's also no Jim. Now Steffi jabs me in the arm and nods with her head toward the back room. And there he is standing in the stockroom talking on the telephone. We're just standing there staring at him when Mr. Howell, the owner of the store, comes waddling over.

"Can I help you girls?" he says, leaning over and trying to catch what we're staring at.

"We—I mean, my friend . . ." Steffi begins, still concentrating on Jim in the back. "Victoria, tell him about the shoes."

"Yeah. . . ." This is going very badly. I certainly don't want Old Man Howell to take my order. But I'm trapped. I can't just stand here like a jerk and not say anything.

"Well, girls . . ." he says.

"Seven-oh-three," I say.

"Hey, Jimmy," he calls to Jim. "Enough with the girl friend already. Get off the phone. I need you."

Jim looks really embarrassed and he quickly hangs up. Steffi pokes me again and says in a stage whisper you could hear four blocks away, "He's coming."

"About time," says Mr. Howell, and before Jim can even get into the front of the store he tells him to go down to the basement and get 703. "What size, honey?" Mr. Howell asks me.

"Six medium." I'm really more like six and a half or even seven, but I hate big feet, and besides, I plan to sell them to Nina anyway.

"In six medium." You can practically hear Jim moan as he heads for the basement to get my shoes. I don't even know him and he hates me already. I'm the jerk who made him drag all the way down to the crummy old cellar to get shoes. And I'm also responsible for making him hang up in the middle of a gorgeous conversation with his grungy girl friend. Well, I'm not sorry about that.

Steffi and I sit down to wait. I'm beginning to think this was a dumb thing to do. I mean, the whole setting is so unromantic with Mr. Howell and this tiny store with all the ugly shoes and Jim having to disappear downstairs. It's all getting very messy. I wish we could get out of here, but we can't with Mr. Howell standing there and just staring at us.

We wait at least a hundred years. Still no Jim. Now Mr. Howell goes to the back steps and calls down. "So Jimmy, huh? Did you fall asleep down there?"

"I can't find any seven-oh-threes, Mr. Howell," he calls back.

"Open your eyes and look near the boiler." This is mortifying.

Silence from the basement.

"So?" says Mr. Howell.

"I don't see them. I'm sorry, Mr. Howell."

"They're right in front of your nose on the side of the boiler."

More silence. I think I want to die. None of this was in my daydreams.

"Aiii, kids. You have to supervise everything. They wouldn't find their head if it wasn't attached." And with a lot of grumbling he goes to the top of the basement steps and shouts down, "Are you at the boiler?"

"Right," Jim shouts up. His voice is beginning to sound not so terrific.

"Now look on the right. You see those stacks of boxes near the window?"

"Yeah."

"So look."

"You want me to look through all the stacks?"

"You got something better to do?"

I hear what is definitely a moan from the basement, and I give Steffi a shove with my elbow and whisper that this is the worst idea in the whole world. "I've ruined everything. How am I ever going to face him again? It's over . . . finished. There's no hope." I'm moaning even worse than he is.

"You're right," Steffi says. She's the most honest friend I've ever had. That's the one thing I hate about her. "Keep your eyes on Mr. Howell," she says. "The minute he turns his head, we disappear."

I give her the gotcha sign and wiggle into my shoes. We get our pocketbooks in our laps and slide to the edge of our seats. But Mr. Howell's not letting go. He keeps us nailed there with his eyes.

There's a lot of noisy shuffling around coming from the basement but still no size sixes.

"You sure you take a size six? Let me measure your foot." And quick as anything he grabs one of those foot measures and advances on us. We both jump up, clutching our bags, and like we were attached start squiggling away from him toward the door. He sort of slides around us and grabs a chair and shoves it into us from behind, pushing us down together on the same seat. Now he whips my shoe off and jams my foot down on the cold metal ruler thing. I guess maybe when you have such ugly shoes in your store you've got to work hard to make a sale. Of course it registers almost seven, but I don't care anymore. As far as I'm concerned my life is over anyway.

"I found them, Mr. Howell! I got them. The size sixes." And Jim comes charging out of the cellar.

Rats! Now he finds them! But it's too late because now Mr. Howell is going to say they're the wrong size and make him go back down and look for the sevens and naturally he's going to think I'm insane and hate me forever.

But it doesn't happen that way. All Mr. Howell says is, "You see what happens when you look with your eyes open?" And he grabs the shoes from the box and pronounces them "perfect, beautiful shoes, are you a lucky girl!"

"I'll put them on," I say, reaching for the shoes.

"No, no, dear, let the boy." And Mr. Howell nods to Jim, who sits down on one of those little seats with the slanted fronts for trying on shoes.

Remember that bit in Cinderella where the mean step-sisters try to squeeze their feet into the glass slipper? That's nothing compared to what goes on with these loathsome espadrilles. Naturally Steffi is absolutely freaking out. She's so hysterical she keeps sliding off the chair and making all kinds of dumb snorting, giggling sounds.

I don't let him give up. I make some excuse about my peds being all bunched up and twist them around, adjust them, pull them up tight, and point my toes with all my might. The espadrilles slide beautifully past the toes and hit a brick wall someplace around the middle of my foot about a mile from the heel. But now my dearest friend, Steffi, is totally convulsed on the floor. The rest of us pretend she's not even in the store.

"I think they're too narrow maybe, huh?" Jim is trying to sound ordinary, like you do with regular normal human beings when they try on shoes that don't fit them.

At this point all I have to say is "Yeah, you're right, too narrow, thanks," or something like that, and pick up my imbecile best friend and walk out. And that's just what I'm about to do but I'm not fast enough.

"Don't worry, dear," Mr. Howell says with a sickly sweet smile, "we'll get you the next size."

We're this little knot of people in one corner of an

almost empty store and there's no way to get away. I see Jim roll his eyes and hear him make a soft groan when Mr. Howell says how he should go back down the basement and find me the right size.

I absolutely cannot let him go back down to the cellar again for shoes I'm never going to put on once I take them out of the store. Besides, he'll despise me forever if I do. So with one horrendous shove, I jam my foot into the shoe, which goes flying into Jim's stomach, pushing him backward right off his seat.

"Perfect," I say through clenched teeth. "I love them snug."

You've got to picture this Keystone Cop bit with Steffi still doubled over on the floor, Jim sprawled down next to her, and me on Jim's seat somehow with my leg sticking straight out in the air. Now Mr. Howell grabs the foot with the new shoe, gives it a this-way that-way squeeze, and pronounces it a perfect fit.

"I'll take them!" I say and start to pull it off. You guessed. It doesn't budge.

"Write up the bill, Jimmy," says Mr. Howell, who's not taking any chances, "while I help the little girl off with her new shoes." And he starts to pull at the shoe.

Jim goes to the cash register to write up the sale. Naturally he's really freaked out because he doesn't know why someone should buy shoes that obviously are miles too small, and any fool can see they are the ugliest, grossest things ever made. How would he possibly know that I'm doing all this out of love for him? All he thinks is that I'm probably on a weekend pass from the nuthouse. Certainly Steffi looks like she is.

"Perhaps you would prefer waiting outside," I say to Steffi in a surprisingly controlled voice while I pinch her arm and nudge her toward the door. She can't exactly answer me, but she obeys and lurches into the street, in screaming hysterics. Very immature.

I, on the other hand, play it absolutely cool. In a flash I see that I can't get the shoe off without a lot of unattractive tugging and puffing, so I say, like it's practically an afterthought, "I think I'll wear it home."

"Here's the other one," Jim says, taking the second shoe out of the box.

"Thanks," I tell him, snapping the shoe out of his hand. "I can manage." He doesn't argue.

With what I hope looks like the greatest of ease, I begin to slip the second shoe on. I'm still toiling at it when Jim begins to wrap up my old shoes. He gives me some long, hard looks. Not those magical electric current things I dreamed about, the kind that pull you together and make everything zing. More like . . . yuck!

Well, nothing is perfect. I'm still working on the shoe when he finishes the wrapping. Now I figure I'll never get the back on, so I just stop trying and crunch down on it. At least I don't have to worry about it sliding off the front—not without a four-man pull team anyway. The worst may be over, so I'm feeling pretty cool. As Jim fills out the sales check, I busy myself studying the net weight on a can of tan Kiwi shoe polish.

"Uh . . . can you give me your name?" Jim says.

Dread moment, but I knew it was coming.

"Regina Goldin Vockwarger." You didn't think I was going to give my real name in a disaster like this, did you?

"Regina what?"

"Goldin Vartbarker."

"Vartwarker?"

"No, Vartrocker." It's the first actual conversation we've ever had, and I want it to last forever.

"Could you spell that, please?"

"Sure. W-A-R . . ."

"W?"

"Yes, V is pronounced W in Hungarian."

"You're Hungarian?" I can tell he's beginning to see

me as a person now. Of course, it's the wrong person, but still . . . it's a start. He's probably saying to himself right now, "Gee, she's not so bad." From out of nowhere Mr. Howell jumps into our private conversation. "Who's Hungarian?" he wants to know.

"She is." Jim motions to me.

"What was that name, darling?" he asks, but I get very busy counting out the money, and as soon as he takes it I scoop up my shoe box and head for the door.

"Vartsugar," I mumble, trying to give a kind of Hungarian warble to my voice. And I open the door fast and zoom out.

The last thing I hear Jim say is, "She's nuts."

I don't know exactly where I screwed up, but I know in my heart it wasn't a total success. Probably more like a horrendous failure that I may never recover from. If only I could go back to where he doesn't know I'm alive.

Steffi comes back to my house and she tries to cheer me up, but I really feel heartbroken because when I looked at him today I knew this was something more than just a kid crush. I think I'm really in love with this beautiful guy, and it probably was dumb and silly and childish to go about it this way. I mean, this is too important for games.

I hope he doesn't remember who I was. But of course he will. *He's* not blind.

Steffi's all for trying it again, this time with a different approach, and she comes up with a couple of other ideas. In one I'm supposed to be taking a survey—you know, one of those house-to-house things, to measure the attitudes of teenage boys toward orphans or something, and the other is a whole big romantic thing where I pretend to faint in his elevator. They're pretty good ideas, especially the fainting one, but I don't know, I'm beginning to think that sort of stuff may be kind of babyish. I don't say that to Steffi because I don't want to insult her, but I don't think I want to spoil what I feel for Jim with some contrived kind of setup. I tell her that if this thing can't start naturally and beautifully I'd rather just keep it inside myself. Of course she understands perfectly. Any best friend would.

Can it be that I'll have to suffer through one of those unrequited loves? That can happen—ugh. Sometimes you just love somebody and nothing can possibly happen. Like with old maids. I guess they probably loved somebody sometime in the past but they weren't loved back, or maybe the guy never knew they existed and so they just spent the whole rest of their lives loving someone from far away.

That's not for me—I mean silently worshiping some idol and just kind of drying up and shriveling away to nothing without him ever knowing.

No way! Okay, so I don't make up some silly little scene. Still, I've made up my mind. I'm not the long-suffering type. I'm not going to tell anyone, not even Steffi. Then it doesn't look so much like a setup, but I intend to make Mr. Jim Freeman very much aware of me very shortly. Watch out, Gloria!

3

Friday night I work on my parents some more about the mother's helper job on Fire Island this summer. I'd be working for Cynthia Landry, this woman who lives in our building. I've been sitting for her kids for almost three years now. Last year she got a divorce. It was really horrendous. David and DeeDee—those are the kids—they were very upset. It's not like you could tell by just looking at them, but it seemed that they were always crying about something. Both of them. They would just burst into tears for nothing. All you had to say was, "David, it's too late to watch TV," or just disagree with him about any little tiny thing, and boom, he would start bawling. It was truly horrific since neither of them are babies. David's almost eight now and DeeDee is five. It could really freak you out, except I knew that it was a reaction to what was happening so I tried to be extra nice. I felt bad for them.

Divorce is such a scary thing. I don't know how you feel, but any time my parents have an argument I practically hold my breath. I guess divorce is the worst thing next to something horrible happening, like one of them dying (I'm very superstitious. I have to knock wood when I even think something awful like that). Just the thought of my father moving away and my mother not loving him, maybe even hating him, makes my stomach sink.

Cynthia hates Jed—that's her ex-husband. He moved to California and he hardly ever sees the kids anymore. When they broke up, people were saying he was playing around with Cynthia's best friend, Amy. I don't know all the juice. All I know is that Amy didn't leave her husband to run off with Jed, but still Charlie the doorman (he knows everything) says Cynthia doesn't talk to Amy anymore, and he says they were practically like sisters. Like Steffi and me, I guess.

It's a funny thing, but I used to think they had a fabulous marriage and I used to baby-sit a lot for them, so I knew what they were like together. It really looked fantastic, I mean they hardly ever argued, and mostly they helped each other and did things together even, like cooking. He liked to mess around in the kitchen and make bread and things like that. I don't know. I even used to hope that my husband (if I ever get married, which I'll probably do when I'm about twenty-seven or so, but I want a career and I want to live with a few people first so I can make the right choice) would be a lot like Jed.

Ugh! He turned out to be such a creep. I don't blame Cynthia for hating him. But that's what makes me so nervous. Not that my parents fight a lot, because they don't. But neither did Cynthia and Jed, and look what happened to them. You can't ever tell what's really going on with your parents. One day they could just come in and announce that it's over, for some dumb reason, like they're incompatible or unfulfilled, and that's that. I mean, there's nothing in the world you can do about it. It's not like a Disney movie where the kids come up with some outrageous plan and then in the end they get the parents back together again. Baloney. It never happens.

Like with Steffi's parents. Everything was great, and then they got a divorce and it looked like there wasn't even any reason. Steffi said there absolutely wasn't anyone else involved, and she and her brother did all sorts of things to try to get them back together, but it didn't make any difference. They had made up their minds. Kids never really have anything to say about family things like that. Whatever your parents decide, no matter how gross or how much it hurts you, forget it, they get to make the decision and that's that. I don't think it's fair at all. But a lot that counts! I mean what a kid thinks.

Anyway, David and DeeDee seem to be pretty okay now. I guess they'll get it together, but still I feel bad for them. I would just love to be their mother's helper for the summer, and I know Cynthia really wants me to be. I freak out just thinking about how sensational it would be living on Fire Island this summer. Not only would I be near Jim, but I'd be practically living on my own. Sure I'd have to take care of the kids, but I don't mind that, and then on my time off I'd be on my own—me and Jim. Oh, I don't think I ever wanted anything so much in all my life!

I have to make my parents understand how much it means to me. My mother is still saying, "We'll see," about the job, but I have to get a definite answer one way or the other soon because if I don't Cynthia is going to get someone else. It just so happens that Steffi's mother said she could go, so if I can't I guess then maybe Cynthia would ask Steffi. I would hate that. I know that's sour grapes and Steffi is really my best friend, but between you and me, I would hate Steffi if she took the job, which of course she would because, after all, why shouldn't she? Naturally I would tell her that I didn't mind, and then she would probably say, "Are you sure?" and I would say, "Absolutely," but I would absolutely hate her and my parents and Nina, too, because she'd probably think it was hysterical that Steffi was getting my job.

No matter how much I want it to be the best, I guess this summer could just possibly be the worst summer of my entire life, which is a pretty awful gift for somebody's fifteenth birthday.

Did I forget to mention that? I turn fifteen on Sunday, and that's when I make my super, final, desperate, dying-gasp plea for the Fire Island job—at my birthday dinner.

I have nothing to wear.

"I have nothing to wear!" I have to scream because I am buried four feet into the bottom of my closet hunting for some scrap of something to wear out tonight for the big dinner with my parents and the gnome, who unfortunately insisted on coming along even though she hates Italian food, especially since I believe I may have mentioned to her sometime or another that it all has squid and octopus in it—alive! She still practically gags at the thought of Italian food, but no, she wouldn't stay home tonight. She knows this is when I plan to talk to my parents about the summer and she wants to make as much trouble as she can. This is going to be a tough fight, all uphill, and I have to look just right, kind of sweet/cute but also old/sophisticated, and I can't find the right dress to wear. It's got to be a good dress, but not my best in case I have to throw myself dramatically out of my chair and pound the dirty floor in a tantrum.

Amazing, I just found a super skirt I haven't seen since I accused my sister Nina of borrowing it and lending it to one of her friends who I was certain had lost it. So, big deal, she didn't. She does enough other awful things, so she could have done this too. Actually if my closet were neater, it would have been hanging up, and then she'd have seen it and certainly would have borrowed it and lent it to her friend, and they're so jerky they absolutely would have lost it so you see I wasn't so wrong in accusing her.

"Victoria, come on, move it! The reservation's for seven-thirty."

My mother is standing in the doorway. I can hear her but I can't see her through all this junk.

I push through all kinds of hanging things, past clumps of dusty shoes, and shopping bags stuffed with scraps of suede from when I was going to make a patchwork skirt, and wool from my crocheting projects, and old letters from summer camp. I'm a saver, sort of. Now I'm peeking through at my mother, who is getting more aggravated than she sounded.

"I have nothing to wear." That wasn't my mother.

"Put on your navy blue dress."

"Gross."

"Or the beige pants. I haven't seen you wear those in ages."

"They're in the laundry."

"Since January?"

"Well, they're at the bottom."

"Ugh." That wasn't me either.

"No jeans, please. This is a good restaurant." And with that irrelevant information, she leaves the room.

Now I want you to know that I'm not just being difficult. I actually have nothing to wear. Sure there's a lot of bulk in my closet but it's all horrendous, Like for example, the navy dress. I can't imagine why I was so crazy to buy it, it's positively disgusting and I look like a giant baby doll in it. My knit skirt hangs down half a mile longer in the back than in the front, and my red dressy sweater itches. Most of my clothes are just nowhere, full of lumps and bumps in all the wrong places, and I'm really in the mood to make a big thing about my wardrobe with my mother, but the plain fact is I can't risk angering her tonight of all nights. She absolutely has to let me go to Fire Island. Period.

I kind of have it worked out in my mind how to do it. We're going to this terrific little restaurant in the Village called Trattoria da Alfredo. The food is out of sight, but the best part about it is that it's very small and sort of quiet. A perfect place to put the squeeze on somebody. I know just how it's going to happen. I start asking them about the mother's helper job, and they're not hot for the idea but I keep at it, and then my father says to lower our voices and we start to whisper loud, and then people start to turn around. You know how adults get very patient with kids when other people are listening? I mean, they just can't say, "I said no, and I don't want to hear any more," like they do at home. They have to pretend to listen and consider it and then give a reasonable answer. I really have them with their backs to the wall, I hope. I'm preparing for an all-out blitz tonight, the kind that takes everyone's appetite away (except, of course, Nina, who could eat through an earthquake).

It happens exactly like I said only a little different. First thing my father says is "No, and I don't want to hear about it anymore."

Of course this is a very bad start, but I push on. I give them the business about how I'm fifteen and they still treat me like a baby. That's an old argument so they know how to answer that easily. Even I know how to answer that. All you say is, "When you can't take no for an answer, that's acting like a baby so we treat you like one."

Then I give them the business about how every other girl in the entire high school is going to be a mother's helper this summer and before they can say anything I rattle off six names ending with Laura Wolfe, the only one I absolutely know is going to.

Up to now the toad has been gorging on fettuccine. Now suddenly she zeroes in to destroy my life. "Uh, uh," says Nina, "Laura Wolfe is going on a camping trip with her parents."

"She is not, smarty, she's going to be a mother's helper for the Kramers out in East Hampton, so there." I could kill her, I swear it.

"Uh, uh." She shakes her dumb head, and the strings of the fettucine hanging out of her mouth swing back and forth.

"She is so!"

"Nope."

"Is so, creep!"

"Ma!"

"Jerk."

"That's enough!" hissed my father. "I don't care what Laura Wolfe or anyone else is doing with her summer."

"But she is, Daddy." I insist. "I know because she said."

"Well, she isn't anymore because her sister, Linda, is in my class, and she said . . ."

"Did you hear your father?" Now my mother's in it. And suddenly the couples at the next table are all dying to hear about Laura Wolfe. "And, Nina, for God's sake, swallow that food. How many times do I have to tell you not to eat spaghetti with half of it hanging down to your chin!"

"I can't help it," she whines, "it just slips out."

"Roll it on the spoon the way I showed you," my father tells her.

"I did."

"If you did it properly it wouldn't fall out of your mouth like that. Do it like this." And my mother starts rolling up a spoonful of spaghetti on her spoon and then pops it into her mouth perfectly. "You see? It's simple. Now let me see you do it."

"I don't have a spoon," says Nina.

"Why are you telling me you rolled it when you don't even have a spoon?"

"I did but it dropped."

Naturally everybody at the surrounding three tables starts hunting for Nina's spoon.

"Ask the waiter for another one," my mother says, embarrassed and completely out of patience.

"I know Laura Wolfe is definitely going." I have to get them back on the track.

"Laura who?" my father says, as if he never heard the name before.

"The girl who's going to be a mother's helper."

"Uh, uh," says my gross sister, and she's got a new batch of spaghetti dripping out of her mouth.

"Shut up!" I tell her.

"How many times do I have to tell you not to say shut up to your sister!" my mother snaps.

"Then make her mind her own business," I say.

"Why do we always have to have these arguments over dinner?" my mother says. "I look forward to a pleasant meal with my family and this is what it turns into."

"Girls," says my father, "enough, you're ruining your mother's dinner. I don't want to hear anything more about Laura Wolfe or what she's doing for the summer. Do you understand?

"And you," he says to Nina. "Don't order spaghetti anymore if you don't know how to eat it."

"But I don't like anything else."

"Then stay home," I tell her.

"Mind your own business, Victoria, I'm talking to Nina," my father says.

"She's always minding my business, and besides just because of her I didn't even get to ask a very important question. It's not fair!"

"Okay, Nina, be quiet," my father says. "Now what's your question, Victoria?"

"Can I?"

"Can you what?" He turns to my mother in exasperation. "Can she what?"

"Can she be a mother's helper," my mother says.

"Well, I don't know." Good sign that my father didn't say absolutely no. "Maybe she's a little young. Maybe next year. What do you think, Felicia?"

Super. He's sticking her with it. Now she can't say, "Your father doesn't want you to," or something like that. It's very bad when you get in the middle of one of those things and then each one keeps blaming the other and you never get the right answer.

"I don't know, Phil, you may be right."

She throws it right back to him.

"If that's what you think, dear."

He grabs it and shoots it back to her. I've got to get it away or they'll just keep passing it back and forth forever.

"Liz started when she was fifteen," I volunteer. Liz is my cousin from Philadelphia, and she really did start last year.

"That's true," says my father, like it's maybe not such a bad idea to do, especially since his favorite sister, Liz's mother, let her do it. "It worked out okay, didn't it?"

"I think so," says my mother.

"It was perfect," I pipe up. "Liz said she really learned a whole lot that summer." You bet she did. But I'm not crazy enough to say *what* she learned.

"Except, now that I think about it," my mother says, "there was some problem about the people leaving her alone for a weekend. I think they went away or something like that. I know Dinah"—my aunt—"was very upset about that. Fifteen-year-old girls shouldn't be left alone with small children overnight."

I swear to them that Cynthia Landry—wonderful, mature, responsible Cynthia—would never go any place and leave me alone with the kids overnight. I tell them how she really needs me because now that she's working she has to have someone with the kids.

"Will she be going into an office every day?" my mother wants to know.

I tell her no, mostly she works from home. But she'll probably be going in to the city maybe about three times a week. And then I make a big thing about how Cynthia and the kids really want me, especially because I've been baby-sitting for them for almost three years and the kids are crazy about me. I can see that they're considering the matter seriously and that it's looking good. Even Nina is minding her own business.

Maybe she ate some octopus. I keep my fingers crossed.

They kick it around awhile, and then they ask me a million questions. Practically Cynthia's whole family history and where on Fire Island and what kind of a house and on and on, and then right in the middle of dessert they decide. Of course, they want to talk to Cynthia and drive out and see the house and all that, but so far the answer is yes.

I practically freak out, I'm so excited. I jump up and hug and kiss both of them. Now the other people and even the waiters are all smiling. Everyone wanted me to go. I almost expect applause, they're all so pleased.

"But . . ."

I knew it! The big "but." Probably my mother will have to come along too, or maybe Nina, or maybe they'll hire a mother's helper for *me* or something grotesque like that, I just know it.

"But," says my mother, "we must be absolutely certain that Mrs. Landry knows that we don't want you to be left alone overnight with the children."

"That's very important, Victoria," my father says. "Mrs. Landry must understand our feelings on that. It's far too big a responsibility for a young girl to have."

"I'll tell her you said so," I say.

"We'll bring it up when we have our talk with her," my father says.

"Please, Daddy, let me tell her."

"I think it's better if we do it ourselves."

"Please, I want to try to handle everything myself. I want her to see that you think I'm responsible enough to make my own arrangements. Then she'll feel better about trusting me."

"That's a good point, honey." Sometimes my dad's absolutely perfect. "She's right, Felicia," he tells my mom. "Let her make her own arrangements. She knows what has to be done."

This was even better than I expected, and I grin like a fool—right at Nina.

Actually talking to Cynthia myself may be a little tricky, because, you know, I don't want to sound like I'm telling her what to do. I can't say to her, "Hey, you can't stay out overnight," like I'm her mother or something. Still, I don't really think she would do it, so it probably won't even come up. If it does—well, I'll just have to figure a way to handle it when it happens. Anyway, it's nothing to worry about now. The main thing is that I'm going. I can't believe it. I'm really going to be on Fire Island with Jim for an entire summer. Wow! Fifteen is going to be a great year!

6

My job is supposed to start on the Friday of the July Fourth weekend, but Cynthia asks me if I'll help them move out on Wednesday. Sure, I tell her, and I can hardly wait to start. I'm supposed to get twenty-five dollars a week and Mondays off. That's probably not a terrific salary but it's great for me. Actually I'd do it for practically nothing just for the chance to be on my own on Fire Island near Jim.

Moving day is really hot, almost 94 degrees, and we're all stuffed into this Volkswagen, and there's no air conditioning, and DeeDee's got poison ivy from the trip to the house last weekend, and she keeps crying how it itches, and Cynthia says don't scratch it. She's got some medicine to put on it but DeeDee says it doesn't help. And every time she scratches it David says, "DeeDee's scratching, Ma," and Cynthia says, "Don't scratch," and DeeDee says, "But it itches," and then ten minutes later they do the whole thing again. It's funny to hear someone else doing the kind of thing Nina and I do. It's not so bad when you're the one doing it, but if you have to just listen, it can drive you up the wall. Then the kids keep asking if we're almost there and can we stop for some kind of Texas hot dog in some special place, and Cynthia says, "We'll see."

But they're not so dumb. They keep asking please because they know what "We'll see" means. I wouldn't mind stopping off for something either, but naturally I can't say anything because I'm the employee, a flunky, sort of, and can't really ask for things. This is the first time in my life I ever worked for anyone like this except baby-sitting, and that's different. You really have to do what your boss tells you, and you can't say, "How come?" or "I'll do it later," or anything. Like when we stop and Cynthia tells me to take DeeDee to the bathroom and then run across the street and get David a candy bar. Or when DeeDee asks for something, Cynthia says, "Victoria will get it." And they're always asking for something—the kids, I mean—and if they don't get it they whine and cry, and DeeDee even once held her breath for God knows how long. I don't remember them doing those kinds of things when I baby-sat for them. And we're not even on Fire Island yet.

Someplace around Bay Shore we have to unload everything and drag it all on the ferry. DeeDee says she can't carry anything because her poison ivy itches. David says he's not going to get stuck carrying everything, and Cynthia says Victoria will carry DeeDee's things. Everyone else makes two trips from the car to the ferry, and I make four, but I don't care because I'm so excited, that I would have carried everything all by myself.

The ferry ride cools us all off. The kids and I sit on the top deck and Cynthia sits downstairs. I put my head back and figure I'll pick up a little quick burn on my cheeks. The air smells salty and the wind whips my hair straight back. I'm going to love this place.

"Victoria," Cynthia calls from the lower deck, "are you watching the children?"

I wasn't but I jump up and search around quickly, and lucky for me they're right there standing at the railing.

"They're okay, Cynthia," I call down the stairs. I sit back down and don't take my eyes off them until fifteen minutes later when we dock. I'm just not used to what I have to do, but I guess I'll learn in a couple of days.

There are no cars allowed on Fire Island so we have
to pile all our stuff on rented wagons—the kind that
kids play with, only bigger. It turns out that no matter
how we arrange it we can't get it all in four wagons, so
we have to leave a load of baggage with the man who
rents the wagons. No problem, Cynthia assures everyone, we'll be able to pick up the rest of the stuff when
we return the other wagons. By now I've got a pretty
good idea who "we" is.

Each one of us grabs a wagon and follows Cynthia
in a line down toward the house.

From the back Cynthia looks like she could be my
age. She's the delicate type, very petite. I'm only five
foot five inches, and she's got to be at least two inches
shorter, and she probably weighs only about 105
pounds, but she's not skinny—she's got a terrific figure. A lot of curves with the tiniest waist. I think she's
very pretty, with greenish gray eyes set wide apart, and
a real short straight nose, not pug. There's nothing
special about her mouth, except that when she smiles
she does show very white straight teeth. What I like
best is her hair. It's dark, dark brown and naturally
curly, and now, in the sun, with all the curls flying
loose, it has a red sparkle. Not that I have any chance
to admire it, not with two kids getting unhappier by
the minute pulling wagons. DeeDee breaks first.

"It's too heavy," she wails from about twenty feet
back.

"Victoria," Cynthia calls to me without stopping,
"please take some of DeeDee's things and see if you
can fit them in your wagon."

My wagon is already the fullest, jammed with all
the heavy things. I couldn't squeeze in another tooth-
pick. I fix it so that DeeDee walks alongside me and I
pull my wagon with one hand and help DeeDee with
the other. I've heard a lot about Fire Island, but this is
the first time I've ever been here. It's not at all what I
expected. We're in a town called Ocean Beach, and it's

fairly well built up, no apartments or hotels, but lots of small wooden houses all close together. There are no sidewalks, only narrow boardwalks and lots of trees and bushes lining the sides.

I love it here already.

"DeeDee, please don't sit in the wagon," I say. "I can't pull you and all the stuff. My arms are breaking." Not only isn't DeeDee helping me pull her wagon but now she wants to ride in it. I have to ask her again nicely please not to. "My arms are breaking. C'mon, DeeDee, please."

"I'm tired . . . and itchy." She pouts. I can see she's going to start crying any second, and I don't want to start anything the first day, so I let her climb on top of the pile of stuff in her wagon. Just when I feel that I can't go another inch, I see Cynthia turn through a creaky old wagon-wheel gate about ten houses up. Dee-Dee jumps off the wagon and runs ahead.

Somehow I drag myself and the two wagons up to the house and collapse on the front steps. I love the place. It's the cutest one on the street, all white shingles with red trimming and geraniums in every single window box. It looks like a dollhouse.

"Victoria, why don't you start carrying in some of the stuff while I make us all some nice cold lemonade," Cynthia says. She leaves her wagon in front of the house and disappears through the front door. The minute she's gone, DeeDee and David shoot off toward the back of the house, and I'm stuck there in the front with four loaded wagons. Nothing to do but start unloading all this junk. Ugh.

"Where should I put these things, Cynthia?" I ask, my arms loaded with clothes.

"David will show you," she calls from what must be the kitchen.

I go back outside and start calling David, but he's nowhere around so I go back into the house to tell

Cynthia. I find her sitting in the kitchen drinking lemonade.

"I can't find David," I tell her.

She looks annoyed right away and asks me did I try the backyard. I say I didn't, but I called loud and he would have heard me if he was anyplace around.

"You can't let them just wander off by themselves," she says to me, getting up and going toward the backyard. She sticks her head out the screen door and calls the kids, and, my luck, they answer right away.

I can see she thinks I didn't look or something.

"I guess they were probably hiding on me." And I smile to show her that it's okay, but she looks like maybe she's wondering if she didn't make a monstrous mistake with me.

"When Victoria calls you, you come, hear?" she tells them.

"We didn't hear anybody calling," David says, shaking his head in all innocence, and DeeDee sees what he's doing and starts to shake her head too.

"I even went outside—where were you?" I ask them.

"It's not important." Cynthia cuts me off. "But next time," she tells them, "you answer when you're called. Now get a move on and help Victoria unload."

"I'm itchy," DeeDee whines. Boy, she better get over that poison ivy quick.

"All right, then don't carry anything. But show Victoria where things go and don't disturb me—I have some important calls to make." And she plops herself down in one of those swivel chairs by the phone and starts dialing.

DeeDee and I go out to get our belongings. David has already brought in his load and dumped it in the middle of the living room. I grab a couple of armfuls and follow DeeDee upstairs. There are three bedrooms on the second floor, all just adorable, freshly painted in sunny colors with starchy curtains on all the windows.

"Where's my bedroom?" I ask DeeDee.

"I'll show you," she says and starts running up another flight of steps. It's a short steep flight and you come up right in the middle of a small room. It reminds me of a tent, and I love it. The ceiling is sloping and sort of low on the sides, but I can stand up almost straight in the center with no trouble. It's a cozy room and not jammed up with a lot of extra things. There's a neat-looking bed with a sort of antique-looking metal headboard and a nice old wooden dresser. I guess maybe it's a little too small to be a dresser, but it's perfect for most of my clothes, and besides, I can hang up the rest in the closet. I don't see a closet, but they have a perfectly good metal rod behind the dresser that gives me plenty of room to hang my stuff, and then I can see exactly what I want without having to bother opening a door. It's a little warm in here now, but that's probably because the window has been shut. It's a nice little window like on a boat, and it doesn't need a curtain or even a shade because it's too small for people to look in, which makes it very private. I love it. I love it all.

"I love the room," I tell DeeDee. "It's so cozy and perfect."

"It used to be a storage closet," she announces and starts downstairs.

"Victoria!" That's my employer calling me, so naturally I answer right away. When my mother is doing it I don't even hear her until the fourth call.

I follow DeeDee down to Cynthia's room. Poor Cynthia is sprawled out on the bed with a wet rag on her head, looking awful. She motions me closer. It's like one of those big dying scenes in the movies.

"Honey, I've got a terrible headache." It seems like an effort for her just to talk.

"Can I get you anything?" I ask.

"Do you want my Teddy to stay with you?" DeeDee asks.

"No, darling." Cynthia manages a weak smile. Then she tells me that she's taken some painkillers and the best thing she can do is rest and try to sleep. Would I please take the kids and go down and get the stuff we left with the wagon man, and while we're there could I please pick up a couple of items from the grocery store.

"Maybe you'd better give them lunch before you go," she says, "and take the dollar on the kitchen table for an ice cream treat for all of you."

"Could I have a double, Mommy?" DeeDee asks.

"We'll leave that to Victoria to decide," she says, and I kind of like that because it shows she trusts my decisions.

"Close the door on your way out, please," Cynthia whispers, sinking fast.

We aren't even down the stairs when DeeDee starts pulling on my jeans.

"Can I?" she asks. "Can I? Please?"

Now that's the big difference between me and a real mother. A real mother would definitely look at her and not have the vaguest idea what she's talking about. "Can you what?" she'd ask. But of course I know exactly what she wants. She's asking about the double scoop. Another thing—Cynthia would certainly say to her, "We'll see," and make it all hinge on how she eats her lunch. But I always hated when my mother would make one thing hang on another, and I swore I wouldn't do that with my own kids, so I might as well start practicing right now.

"Absolutely," I tell DeeDee. "You can have whatever two flavors you want."

Naturally the kid's stunned.

I find David and fix them both tuna sandwiches. David wolfs his down in two seconds, but DeeDee just sits there staring at hers.

"Come on, DeeDee." I coax her. "At least finish half."

"I don't want to," she says, shoving it away from her.

"Do you want something else?"

She shakes her head. "I'm not hungry."

Naturally I could threaten to take away the second ice cream, but what for? That'd be just what mothers always do, and I want to try out some of my own ideas about raising kids.

"Are you sure you're not hungry at all?" I ask her one last time.

"Uh, uh, I'm all fulled up."

You have to trust what a kid says; after all, she knows if she's hungry or not better than I do. "Okay," I tell them, "then let's get going."

We get the empty wagons and David shows me how to pile them all on my wagon. We start walking toward the docks. I can see that DeeDee is unhappy. I think it's because she wants a ride, so I ask her if she wants to sit in the wagon, but she shakes her head no.

"What's the matter, DeeDee? Come on, you can tell me."

"Am I still going to get the ice cream?" she asks, about a millimeter away from tears.

"Of course you are. Just like I promised. A double scoop." Poor kid's not used to trusting mother figures. I'm going to be the best mother in the whole world.

"I want it now."

"It'll taste better when you're hungry."

"But I *am* hungry." Instantly her nose is red, and the tears are streaming down her cheeks. "I didn't have any lunch," she wails.

I think I've been had by a five-year-old. "Okay, okay. . . ." What can I do? I really did promise.

"Now," she says, all smiles, "you said I could ride on the wagon. Put me on."

I'll get her.

The little monster climbs up on the wagon and off

we go toward the ice cream shop. It's down near the
ferry dock. All the action is around there. Cute bou-
tiques and grocery stores and even a pizza place. I keep
my eyes open for The Dunes, the place where Jim
works, but I don't see it. David and DeeDee never
heard of it, but that's probably because they're too little.

The ice cream is sensational, best I ever had, but I
guess the price must have gone up since last year because I have to kick in fifty cents. I don't mind,
though, especially since I know Cynthia's having a terrible money problem. She's trying to sell the Fire Island house, and I heard that they may have to move
from their apartment in the city. Everyone says it's because Jed doesn't pay anything. He's truly disgusting
to walk out the way he did and then not send money,
not even any for the kids. That really stinks. I feel
very bad for Cynthia.

We return the other wagons to the rental place and
pick up the one we had to leave there. Another ferry is
pulling in and the kids want to watch, so we walk out
on the pier. And then I hear a guy's voice not two feet
behind me say, "Hi, Victoria."

7

It's Barry, that guy I told you about, the one who's always staring at me, from school, Jim's friend.

"Oh, hi, Barry," I say, giving my mouth a quick wipe for any stray cone crumbs, pulling in my stomach, smiling, and trying inconspicuously to notice if Jim is anywhere around. With another couple of seconds I could do a fast fix on my hair, which probably looks like rat tails hanging from my head. But I guess it's okay, because I don't see Jim around anyway.

"Hey," Barry says, coming over to us, "I didn't know you were going to be out here." And he looks so nice and smily that I think it's not going to be hard making friends with him. Actually, he's a lot cuter than I thought he was in school. Maybe it's that terrific tan he's got. It goes great with his wavy black hair. He just looks different out here. I always thought of him as a string bean, kind of tall and skinny, but he's not really skinny, he's slim, and he's got a fairly nice build. Don't get me wrong; he's far from gorgeous—his nose is a little biggish and his smile doesn't dazzle like Jim's, but his eyes are soft brown and friendly, and he's got a shy, sweet look about him that makes me feel totally relaxed.

Another thing, Jim is so perfect that I sometimes think I would probably feel kind of clunky next to him, but with Barry I feel pretty. Prettier than Barry, anyway.

A wide grin crosses his face and he asks, "How long are you here for?"

"All summer," I say. "I'm a mother's helper."

"No kidding. Are those the victims?" He winks at David and DeeDee.

"Right," I say, and introduce him to the kids.

"How do you do, David," he says, solemnly shaking DeeDee's hand, and she practically falls down giggling. And then David gets into it and shakes Barry's hand and says he's DeeDee, and then Barry says no, *he's* DeeDee, and then I get into it and we're all bowing and shaking hands, and the kids are hysterical, and in two seconds we're all old friends. He's cute. Barry, I mean. Nice cute.

I don't want him to know how much I know about him, so I have to ask him what he's doing out here, and then he tells me all the things I already know and one extra. The best one. That ferry I mentioned? The one that's just about pulling into the slip right this minute? Well, Jim is on it. How's that for timing?

Now of course, I've got to find a way to fix my hair. Inconspicuously. I don't want Barry to think it's because of Jim.

"DeeDee, honey," I coo to her, wiggling my finger for her to come. "I just want to fix your hair a little," I tell her. Of course she's going to say no, and then I'll tell her, "See, I'm going to fix my hair too."

"Okay," she says, screwing up the whole plan.

It's too late to change plans, so like a fool I add, "See, I'm going to fix my hair too."

"So what?"

"And then I'll fix your hair."

"I wanna go first."

"And so you will." I smile down at her, frantically brushing my hair. "Right after me, you go first."

She's so confused she doesn't even make a fuss.

"Look," I tell the kids, "the ferry's docking."

The four of us stand there, watching the people

coming off the boat. Everyone is loaded down with tons of luggage and backpacks and things. It's the opening of the season, and people with houses are moving all their things out. My heart is practically pounding out of my chest knowing I'm going to see Jim. I'm getting worse every day.

There he is. And . . .

"There they are." Barry pokes me to look at my Jim leaving the ferry with this horrendous growth hanging off his left arm. Barry waves at them.

"Hey! Jimmy! Gloria! Over here!"

"I didn't know Gloria was coming out here too," I say very casually.

"She's just here for the day," Barry says, and looks at me kind of surprised. "Don't you like her?"

"Are you kidding? I think she's . . . she's . . . something else." I'm smart enough not to say what. Actually I despise her type of girl—as I told you—the cutesy cheerleader kind with the slippery blonde hair that hangs a mile down their backs and the dimples that simply look like cheek holes to me.

A lot of the little kids in school are impressed just because Gloria is captain of the cheerleaders. They think she's a real big deal, and at the ball games you're always hearing them saying did you see what Gloria did with her hair, or get a load of those boots Gloria's wearing, or something about her eyes. You'd think she was the only person in the world to have blue eyes. In my opinion, one look in those eyes and you think nobody's home.

Anyway, here they come. I don't think Jim's going to recognize me from the shoe store because, after all, there are probably lots of customers going in all the time. Why should he just remember me? I wasn't in there that long, and most of the time he was down in the basement anyway. I hope like crazy he doesn't remember me. I don't think I was at my best that day.

"Gloria?" Barry grabs one of Jim's bags from her.

Obviously *he* doesn't think nobody's home behind those eyes. "Do you know Victoria Martin? Victoria, do you know Gloria Donovan and Jimmy Freeman?"

And like I never laid eyes on either of them before this minute, I say, "Hi." Please, God, don't let him recognize me.

"Hi," Jim says, and he does one of those double takes and looks kind of puzzled, but I keep very cool and look at him like I'm a completely new person. I give him a wide, open kind of smile—slightly upturned face, merry eyes, absolutely nothing to hide. It works. I can practically hear him saying to himself, "Naaw, that can't be that nut from the shoe store."

As for Gloria the Magnificent, she can't even squeeze out a "hi." All she can manage is a sickly dumb smile with those stupid cheek holes. Naturally every tooth is perfect.

"How's it going, buddy?" Jim says to Barry, giving him one of those affectionate back slaps.

"Okay," Barry says, "still pretty quiet, though."

"But picking up a little, right?" Jim kind of motions in my direction. At least I think that's what he's doing. Obviously Barry does, too, because he gets real embarrassed-looking and says, "Yeah, I guess so."

And Gloria looks annoyed. Super! I guess he did mean me.

"Been getting in any tennis?" Jim asks, and Barry says he's been waiting for him, and Jim says, "Well, buddy, here I am."

And that's the feeling you get, that it's all about to start because *here he is*. Jim is definitely a mover type, and people like to move with him. Like now, with Barry, Jim's the one who sets the time and date for their tennis game even though it's Barry's court. But that's the way it is, Jim calls the shots, and people just kind of want to go along with him.

Everyone's always talking about how some politicians have charisma. Well, I'm not exactly sure what it is—charisma, I mean—but the way everyone is so attracted to Jim I think he must have tons of it.

"Victoria . . ." DeeDee is sniffling and tugging at my shorts. "My ice cream is melting all down."

"Who is *that*?" Gloria says, looking at DeeDee like she was some kind of bug. I admit she looks pretty disgusting with chocolate ice cream all over her face and running down her arm and dripping off her elbow. Still, I don't like Gloria's tone.

"That's DeeDee," Barry says, "if you can find her under all that ice cream. Victoria's a mother's helper."

"Who are you working for?" Suddenly Gloria is all interested.

"Cynthia Landry," I tell her.

"I know her!" she squeals.

"Come on, DeeDee," I say, paying no attention to Gloria, who obviously can't wait to unload on Cynthia. "I'll wash you off in the water fountain."

"No," she says, "I want to do it myself."

The fountain is a few feet away, so I let her do it herself.

Gloria can't hold it in. "Boy," she chirps, "poor Cynthia. She had a real rat husband who played around with everyone and ran off to California. Was he gorgeous! Looked like Al Pacino."

Gross! No wonder Cynthia hates Jed. It's horrendous to think everyone knows your whole life's story and how your husband was playing around. He really was disgusting. And so is Gloria for gossiping around like that.

"That's what a lot of people are saying." I sniff. "But of course they don't know the real story, so they just keep repeating the old gossip."

That ought to fix her wagon.

"Far out! I'd just love to know the whole story," she says. She's so dumb she doesn't even know when she's being put down. How can Jim stand her?

"Hey, the Landry house is in Ocean Beach too," she

says, and then turns toward Jim. "Isn't that nice," she
purrs, giving him a brilliant smile. "You'll be real
close neighbors."

"I don't know how close we'll be," I say as noncha-
lantly as I can manage.

"Well, I do," she says, really snotty. "The Landrys'
house is on Evergreen, right around the corner from
Jimmy boy's. Actually, Cynthia offered *me* the job
this year, but I said no. I would have considered it if
gorgeous Jed was still there, but I make it a policy
never to work for divorced women. They stick you
with the kids twenty-four hours a day because they're
always running around. Besides," she says, sending the
last bullet directly into my brain, "she was paying peanuts."

"That's really super!" Barry cuts in. What's super?
That she's paying me peanuts? "All three of us are
going to be together this summer," he continues, and
he's really excited. Jim doesn't dare say a word with
Gloria staring at him.

"It sounds so cozy, maybe I should plan to spend a
little more time out here too." Gloria says that last
line right in my face. God, I loathe her!

"Jimmmmmy." There goes Gloria the whiner again.
"I'm positively exhausted. I simply must get to the
house. Are you coming?"

"Yeah, sure," Jim says, grabbing up his gear. Then
he says to me, "You know, I know you from somewhere."

"It must be from school," I say weakly. I'm in abso-
lute, stark terror.

"No, not school," Jim says thoughtfully. "Maybe
with Barry. Or—no. . . ."

He'll never let go.

"Jim-my!" Gloria whines.

"Okay . . ." he says. "I was just trying to figure out
how I know Barry's girl friend."

Barry's girl friend! That's disaster if he thinks I'm

Barry's girl friend. I have to set him straight right now.

"I think there's some misunderstanding . . ." I want to do it gently because after all he is Barry's friend, and besides, I don't want to hurt Barry. "Barry and I . . ."

"Jimmy, c'mon . . ."

"Okay . . ." he says, but he's still looking at me.

". . . I'm hungry."

"Hungry!" he says like he just discovered the wheel, and points to me.

"No, thank you. I just ate. Well, I'll see you all around sometime," and I grab DeeDee and call David, who's been lost in a comic book all this time, and take about two giant steps when a hand grabs my shoulder.

"You're the Hungarian who went home with tight shoes!" Jim is on the other end of that hand.

"The Hungarian?" Barry and Gloria say it together like a vaudeville act.

"Oh, man, you should have seen her and her friend. . . ." And he practically doubles over in hysterics. He starts laughing so hard he can barely tell the story. Frankly, I didn't think it was funny at all.

Finally he gets the whole story out, and the three of them are cracking up. I ask, kind of cold, "What's so funny about being Hungarian?"

"Hey, nothing . . . we weren't laughing because you're Hungarian. . . ." And he practically falls on the ground, he's laughing so hard.

Anyway, one thing and another and they finally pull themselves together and Jim grabs his stuff, which of course had fallen all over during his little story.

"Hey, see you around," Jim says to me. Then to Barry, "You really picked yourself a winner, chum," and he chuckles good-naturedly.

I can do without the whole thing. I am not Barry's girl friend. "I am *not* Barry's girl friend," I say to all three. "I practically only met Barry for the first time today. So I couldn't possibly be Barry's girl friend, and furthermore I'm not even Hungarian. My friend is."

And as if it didn't matter at all, Jim and Gloria say, "Sure, that's terrific," or something like that. "See you later," they say, and while my brain is seething, the love of my life takes off with the love of his life, and I'm left alone with David, DeeDee, who just dropped her cone on my left shoe, and lover boy Barry.

"You shouldn't tell people I'm your girl friend. That's ridiculous, we only practically just met." I'm not trying to sound angry, but I'm really ticked off.

"I didn't exactly say you were my girl friend, more like . . . that . . ." I hate to make him struggle like that, but, damn, it's not *fair*.

"More like what?"

"That . . . you know . . . more like I liked you."

Well, I can't exactly hang him for liking me. At least someone does.

"Actually . . ." Now he's really stammering. "It's more than that. More like. . . ."

Now I'm the one staring at him.

". . . I love you."

Unreal!

"You can't love me!"

"But I do."

"But you can't!" I know this is a ridiculous argument, but he can't. "You hardly even know me."

"I know you better than you think. I've been watching you all year."

See, I told you he was always following me around and staring at me.

"And I know I'm deeply in love with you."

Oh, God, he's deeply in love with me. Is he crazy or something?

"I think you're the most beautiful girl in the entire school."

He's really making me nervous now.

"I can't think of anyone but you. You've become the most important person in my life."

And when I get nervous . . .

"We have to be together."

. . . I laugh.

And of course I crack up. I know it seems like the meanest thing in the world, but I swear I'm not laughing at him, I'm just laughing because I'm nervous and I can't handle the situation. It's horrible but he naturally thinks I'm laughing at him. Now he grabs me by the shoulders, and his face is two inches from mine, and he looks crushed, and I feel terrible and I want to cry but I can't stop laughing. I try to tell him that I'm not laughing at him, but every time I open my mouth to get the words out I become so hysterical I can't talk. All I can manage is half of "I'm sorry," which he probably can't even make out.

Now he turns away from me, and I'm afraid he's going to cry. Just like that, the laughing jag disappears and I'm back in control. First thing I tell him is that I'm sorry and that I wasn't laughing at him, I just wasn't expecting anything like that and he threw me, and more "I'm sorry"s and "please forgive me"s and "I feel horrible," but it's like he didn't hear anything because when he turns back to me he's really angry.

"Forget it. It's my problem." And he starts to walk away.

"No, wait." I grab his arm. "I really am sorry. Please . . ."

"I told you, forget it. It was a mistake. I shouldn't have told you. What a jerk I was." And I can see he's really hurt. If I can love Jim without knowing him, why can't Barry love me? Then I think, suppose I told Jim and he laughed in my face . . . I think I'd just die. Oh, God, I feel horrible. He shakes my hand off his arm. I keep apologizing, but it's too late.

"Don't tell me how you're so sorry, just don't tell me anything. I suppose you think it's funny . . . well, it isn't. It hurts . . . it hurts a lot." And while he's still talking, he starts to walk away.

"Please, wait . . ."

"Good-bye."

And he's gone.

I feel like a monster. I absolutely hate myself, and now I'm the one who feels like crying. I'm so ashamed.

"I'm sorry . . ." DeeDee puts her arms around my legs and kisses my kneecaps, "I didn't mean it. I'll never do it again."

I bend down to ask her what she did, but all she does is shake her head and look as if she's going to cry. Boy, we're a great group today.

I ask her again and this time she says she doesn't know.

"Then why are you sorry?" I ask.

"Because," she says, "I don't want you to cry."

Oh, God, she thinks I'm upset because of her. Naturally I hug her and tell her she has nothing to do with it and besides everything is fine now and I feel great. Funny, isn't it? When you're little like that you think everything that happens has to do with you. I can remember when I was really young, if I heard my parents arguing in their room I was always certain it was about me.

We pick up the things from Cynthia's list at the grocery and the drugstore and start back to the house.

All the way home I can't help but feel miserable about what happened with Barry. I swear I'm going to make it up to him somehow. I can't love him, you know. If you don't love someone you just can't make yourself. But at least I'll show him that I appreciate the way he feels about me and that I understand and that it makes him really special to me . . . always. I'm absolutely going to spend the whole summer making it up to him. Not that I expect it to take the whole summer.

Still, you have to realize it's only partly my fault

that it worked out so bad. After all, that was a heavy thing to lay on someone, especially when they didn't expect it at all. It's not my fault he fell in love with me. I certainly didn't make him do it. I didn't even know he was doing it. Sure, I shouldn't have laughed, but you take your chances when you spring something like that on someone you hardly know. And then that part about letting Jim think I was his girl friend—that really bugs me. That was really gross of him—not that I'm saying what I did was right—still, he wasn't so right himself.

Even so, he's really a pretty nice guy, and it would be nice to be his friend. Not only because of Jim, but because he's definitely a nice person with a good sense of humor and cute and . . . I don't know, he's just a good type to have for a friend.

On the way home David sees one of his friends and wants to go back to his house, but I have to say no because I don't know if I have the authority to let the kids go off on their own like that. David gets a little aggravated and starts crying, and then DeeDee says something, and he kind of kicks her, not a bad one, only on her shoe, but she gets hysterical. It's sort of embarrassing because I think everyone thinks I probably hit them, and of course I would never touch them, ever.

I try to explain to David that it's my first day and I don't really know the rules but he's going to be there for the whole summer and there'll be other times and so on, and I almost feel like a mother. I know I sound like one. What's really funny is that I think someone said something just like that to me a couple of years ago at camp. I don't remember what the situation was, but I know it didn't help then and it doesn't help now. All the way home David won't even talk to me.

Turns out he could have gone with his friend, which even makes him angrier, but I was afraid to take the chance. But everything gets better anyway because I play a couple of games of War with David, and Sorry with DeeDee, and then the three of us play Monopoly, and then DeeDee gets upset about losing and throws the board into the air and all the pieces go flying. David runs off to tell his mother, who says it's time for Dee-Dee's bath anyway, and to me, "Victoria, see that they put that game away properly, please." Suddenly David gets a bad stomachache and has to go to the bathroom, and DeeDee goes up to get ready for her bath. It doesn't take me that long to pick up the pieces, and by the time DeeDee is ready for me to shampoo her hair I've finished. The game will never be the same. When the kids are in their pj's, Cynthia says they can watch TV until eight and then to bed.

I figure that later on, after they're in bed, if Cynthia isn't going out I'll take a walk down to the dock and see what's doing. It probably takes a while longer for my room to cool off because it gets the afternoon sun, so it's still a little warmish up there, but that's okay because by the time I'm ready for bed it will probably be perfect. I throw myself together a little bit and go downstairs. Cynthia is on the phone so I just sit down and grab a magazine and wait.

"That's out of the question," she's saying. "No!" She sounds furious. I hope it isn't about me. Whoops, I sound just like DeeDee. "Absolutely not, Henry. I won't permit you to see them and I don't want you to call anymore. . . . I certainly can, they're my children. . . . He's your son, you see what you can do with him."

Of course, it has to be about her ex-husband, Jed. Maybe she doesn't want the kids to see him.

"Well," she snaps, "until he does there's nothing more to say. Please don't call here anymore." And she hangs up.

"Damn bastard!" she says, and I hear her throw something like a pencil against the wall. Well, at least it wasn't about me. I figure now's not the time to ask to go out, so I just sit there pretending to be reading. Finally she sits down next to me. She's still angry.

"If Henry Landry—that's the children's grandfather—calls I don't want you to let him talk to them."

"You mean you don't want me to let the kids talk to their grandfather?" It's not like I mean to question her, it's just that I want to be absolutely sure what she wants me to do. Because, after all, it is their grandfather.

"That's right. You just tell him they're not home and that I said not to call anymore."

"Even if they are home?"

"Yes, Victoria, the whole point is that I don't want him to be in touch with them at all. At least not until his son pays some of his bills."

"Oh, I see." But I really don't. I can't believe she's not going to let the kids speak to their own grandfather. That's horrendous.

"I suppose as long as you're going to be involved in this mess you should understand it a little better." And then she tells me how Jed took off for California (of course, she doesn't say anything about how he was playing around) and how he never even calls the kids and now he's even stopped sending money. She does design displays for stores, but it doesn't pay all that much money, and now they're going to have to sell the house on Fire Island and the kids really love this place. Worse than that, she thinks she'll have to move out of the city because it's too expensive, and then it means she'll have to do more traveling to her job and she won't be able to spend as much time with the kids, and now that they don't have a father they need her even more than ever.

"I suppose we really shouldn't have even come out this summer," she says, "but I knew it would be the last time for the children on Fire Island, and they suffered so much this past year I wanted to give them the best summer I could." She looks so sad.

"That's really terrible." I say. "I mean him not helping out at all. It's like he doesn't care."

"He's impossible, and the truth is he really doesn't care."

"Can't you make him pay? Take him to court or something?"

"It's very hard because he's way out in California. If he were in New York I could haul him into court and they would make him pay. They have ways of taking part of his salary. I've talked to him, pleaded with him, everything, but all he does is hang up on me. I know his father has some influence over him, so I thought if I refused to let Henry—that's his father— see the kids, even if Jed wouldn't do anything for his children, at least he would do something for his father. I'm hoping Henry will be able to do something with Jed. Henry is very fond of the children, but I feel he's also somewhat responsible for his son's behavior. I don't know. . . ." She puts her head in her hands, and I know she's trying hard not to cry in front of me. "Maybe it's not the best way, but I've tried everything else. . . . Anyway"—now she sort of pulls herself together—"that's what I want you to do. If Henry calls, tell him no and not to call anymore. If he gives you any trouble just hang right up."

It blows my mind just thinking about hanging up on somebody's grandfather. I could never in the whole world hang up on my grandfather, and I would hate anyone else who did. Maybe if I just let the kids answer the phone . . .

"What if David or DeeDee picks up the phone?" I better straighten this out right away.

"I'm going to tell them not to answer the phone."

"But won't they want to know how come?"

"I'll deal with that. In the meantime I don't want them to know anything about what I told you. Victoria, I'm sure you understand how important it is that they don't know even one thing about the situation. They're much too young—they'd never understand."

"I won't say anything, I swear."

"I'm counting on you."

I just know I'll freak out if he calls. What a drag. I guess she sees it on my face because she says, "Don't worry about it, Victoria—he's probably not going to call anymore. After all, I asked him not to, and he's a pretty decent man. A lot better than his son, I might add."

"I guess he probably won't," I say, but I know I'm going to die every time the phone rings.

"Listen, honey, I'm going out for a while. After a day like today I need a little relaxation . . . moving day is always a nightmare. But you were a great help. You did a terrific job."

"Thanks."

"No, thank *you*."

I told you she was a terrific person. We really get along sensationally. "By the way," I ask, "do you know where The Dunes is?"

"Sure, it's just past Ocean Beach toward Cherry Grove. That's where I'm going tonight."

"You are?" I ask, a little surprised.

"Yes, it's a bar and a restaurant, and sometimes they turn it into a disco. Everybody goes there. But I think the crowd is a little old for you."

"Oh, no, I wasn't planning to go, I just know someone who's working there. He's a waiter."

But Cynthia won't let go of the subject. "Well, where do you know him from?" she asks.

"From the city," I answer. I really wish she'd drop it.

"The city. I see. Victoria, please sit down for a minute. There's something I want to discuss with you."

I know a lecture's coming. God knows why, but I know it in my bones. Naturally I sit right down. I hope I have a tissue in my pocket in case she makes me cry.

"Don't look so scared. There's nothing wrong."

It's worse than I thought.

"I only wanted to give you a little advice. I know this is your first time on your own and problems are bound to come up, so I want you to know that you can come to me any time about anything. Kind of look on me as your summer mother. Okay?"

"Sure, that'd be great." I told you she's really very nice.

"Another thing. While you're living with us you're my responsibility and I take that very seriously. So remember, if I'm your summer mother that makes you my summer daughter, and I think I'd better warn you about something. There are two discos out here, The Dunes and The Monkey, and they're both really a couple of years too old for you. Especially The Monkey. I know a lot of teenagers go there. But it's a pretty raunchy place, if you want the truth. Anybody who goes in there is expected to know the score—if you follow me. So be careful about that place. Be careful about where you go and who you see and everything like that, okay? And one last thing—your curfew. It's pretty safe out here as far as crime goes, this being an island and all, so I think your curfew can be a little later. How's one o'clock on the weekends?"

"Terrific!"

"Okay, that's set. But please remember I expect you to be on time."

"Oh, I will. I promise."

"All right them, that's it. I'm off. Watch TV if you like, or I have a new *Vogue* in my bedroom if you want, and if you get a chance, could you please throw in a laundry? The whites are separate and don't put any sweaters in the dryer. Thanks a lot. You're a doll." And she's off.

It's okay that I'm not going tonight. I look gross anyway. I have to wash my hair, and besides, I'm really exhausted. I get the laundry from upstairs. Turns out to be two big laundry bags full. I guess Cynthia's been so busy getting packed and ready to go she didn't have a chance to do anything else. I don't mind doing laundry—it's an easy job. I separate the whites and colors, and it looks like maybe four loads. I probably have time to do most of them. I'd like to do something really terrific my first day so I start putting in the laundry and by about one a.m. I've finished all the laundry, washing, drying, and folding everything except the stuff that has to be ironed. I pile everything on the couch and chairs in the living room and go off to bed.

It's still very hot in my room, but that's because it's especially hot tonight. But I'm too tired for it to matter, and next thing I know it's morning and DeeDee is crawling in my bed.

8

"C'mon, Victoria, let's go to the beach." DeeDee is pulling on my arm, but for a minute I don't even know where I am. Then I remember.

"What time is it?" I mumble.

"The big hand is on the four and the little hand is right next to the seven, but not on it yet."

I work it out and groan. "Oh, God, it's twenty after six. DeeDee, it's too early, go back to bed."

"I don't want to. I'm hungry. Mommy says you're supposed to fix me breakfast and I'm hungry."

"But it's not even seven." I'm trying to be reasonable and nice at the same time. Very hard so early in the morning.

"But I'm hungry." DeeDee is being neither.

"Okay, five minutes more."

"Now!"

Monster. I sit up, bumping my head on the ceiling. I guess it's a little lower on the sides than I thought. It takes me a while to get up and get it all together. With my eyes half shut I creep downstairs and into the kitchen.

"What do you eat for breakfast?"

"Pancakes."

"Forget it! What else?"

"Or eggs and bacon or sometimes Mommy even makes waffles. . . ."

"What else?"

"I dunno . . . cereal, I guess."

"That's it." And I go to the pantry and pull out three different kinds of dry cereal.

"I want Sugar Pops!"

Naturally we don't have any Sugar Pops. I try to sell her on one of the others, but she only wants the dumb Sugar Pops, so I fix her scrambled eggs, which she pushes around on her plate until they finally slip into her lap. That's the end of breakfast. I guess she wasn't so hungry after all.

"Why don't you watch some TV for a while and then we'll get dressed and go to the beach."

"I can't."

"Why not?"

"There's no room to sit," she says, pointing to all the laundry still piled up all over. I guess Cynthia got home too late to bother with it. I clear a little spot for DeeDee and put on the TV and sneak upstairs to get back to bed, but David hears me, and now he wants his breakfast, and we go back down and go through the whole breakfast thing, only he insists on a peanut butter sandwich and swears he has one every morning.

No point in going back to bed, so I get into my bathing suit and straighten up my room. I tell the kids that if they want to go to the beach they have to make their beds. They both say they don't have to make their beds. Then we have this little thing about how their mommy never makes them make their beds so why should I. I guess they're right, so I make their beds while they get into their bathing suits, and we all head down to the beach.

The beach is fabulous, with white clean sand and roaring white water, and absolutely empty except that way down you can see someone who looks like maybe he's fishing. David takes off as if he was shot out of a cannon and races across the sand and plunges right into the water. Brrr!

"Wow!" I say to DeeDee. "Does he always do that?"

"Uh-uh, my mommy never lets him go in the water like that unless a grown-up is with him."

"Oh, God!" I shoot down after him. I race into the water even though it's unbelievably freezing. He's already over his head. I can see he's a pretty good swimmer for a little kid, but still he's way too far out, so I call him and wave my arms, and I know he sees me but he doesn't pay any attention. So I have to swim after him. When I get close enough, and I'm really angry now, I call him and tell him to get right back in shore. Now! He says something that sounds like, "Aw, shit," and heads back.

"You're never to go in the water without me!" I scold him. "You understand? I'm not kidding around either." He really scared me, so I'm sort of sharp with him.

"I thought you were coming with me." He's so full of it.

"I didn't even know you were going. Come off it, David, just don't do that again. Next time you want to go in the water, tell me first so I can go with you."

"I want to go now."

"Well, you have to wait. We're not even settled yet—besides, I want to sit down and warm up a little in the sun."

"When can I go?" he asks.

"In a few minutes," I tell him, and DeeDee helps me spread the blanket down. The minute I lie down, David wants to know if we can go swimming again. Then every sixty seconds, like clockwork, he says, "Now?" It's hopeless.

"Let's collect some shells and then we'll go. How's that?"

"I wanna, I wanna." DeeDee jumps up.

"C'mon, David," I say, and I get up, brushing the sand off me. David has been jumping around so much that the sand was flying all over. He didn't do it purposely but it's all in my hair.

"Then can we go swimming?" he asks, and I tell him absolutely. We head down the shoreline toward the fisherman, our heads bent as we look for treasures. Every time DeeDee finds any kind of shell she has to show me. I can tell she really likes me. And I like her, too, except I think that maybe they're both a little spoiled. Still, she's really very cute, with blond curly hair and chocolate-brown eyes. She's got the kind of lips that look like she's wearing lipstick, they're so rosy. Her cheeks too. She's truly adorable, and I think she knows it.

As we get closer to the figure on the shore, we can see that he *is* fishing.

"My grandpa is the best fisherman in the whole world," David says, and for the first time since we left New York DeeDee agrees with him.

"And sometimes he even takes us fishing with him," says DeeDee, "and then we catch great big fish." And she spreads her arms as wide as they will go.

"You never caught a big fish," David says, and she says, "I did too," and he says, "You did not," then they do that uh-huh, uh-uh thing, and I start pointing at the fisherman and shouting, "I think he's got one!"

I don't really think he's got one, but I have to change the subject. As soon as we get up to the man, DeeDee tells him how her grandfather is such a great fisherman, and the man is very nice, and he smiles and says he bets he is, and then the three of them gab on about fishing and the kids really seem to know what they're talking about. Even DeeDee. They must have spent a lot of time with their grandfather, which makes me feel bad since they're not going to be allowed to see him or even talk to him. I know that Cynthia's right to be angry because her ex-husband is really a creep, but maybe it's wrong for her to take it out on the grandfather. After all, it's not his fault that his son is so disgusting. At least I don't think it is, or maybe Cynthia's right, maybe the old man can do something to make Jed start paying again. I don't know, but it makes me feel awful, I mean really sad, and not just for the kids but for the grandfather too. I can just imagine how my grandpa would feel if he wasn't allowed to see Nina and me.

The fisherman lets David and DeeDee hold the line for a few minutes, but they don't get anything, and after a while we walk back to our towels.

"He's okay," David says, nodding back at the fisherman. "But my grandpa is much better. My grandpa woulda caught maybe ten fish by now, right, Dee-Dee?"

"Yeah, maybe eleven. Do you know my grandpa?" DeeDee asks me.

"I don't think I ever met him," I say, and then just because I want to change the conversation I ask David if he wants to go swimming. The water's great to look at but it's freezing. Still, even that's better than talking about their grandfather.

I can see David's a terror in the water. You have to watch him every second because right away he goes too far out, and then it's unreal when you tell him that's enough swimming for now. His lips turn bright blue, but still he says he's not cold, and then he pretends not to hear you, and then the worst is when he makes believe he's drowning. First time he did it I almost jumped out of my skin. I swam out to him with all my might and grabbed him and started pulling at him, not exactly like in the lifesaving class at school but good enough to get him back to shallow water, and then he starts laughing like crazy and I could have *really* drowned him. I told him that if he ever did that again I would tell his mother and he wouldn't go in the water for the whole summer, and besides I would quit. I was really freaked out. In fact, I was practically in tears. I guess he saw how upset I was because he swore he would never do it again. I made him swear to God and cross his heart on his mother's life and all that, and I made sure he didn't have any fingers crossed, and I think maybe he means it.

At about noon we head back to the house for lunch. There's a note from Cynthia saying not to disturb her because she has a headache. I hope she's not coming down with anything, because that's what happens to me when I get sick. Sometimes I start off with headaches. Anyway, the note says I should give the kids lunch, put the laundry away, and then there's a list of things for me to pick up at the store.

I give the kids tuna salad sandwiches and do their dishes and whatever was left from Cynthia's in the sink.

After I put the laundry away (the kids tell me where everything goes) we all go down to the dock where the stores are to do the shopping. DeeDee tells me her mother always takes the wagon to the store, and the list is pretty long so I take one. Naturally Dee-Dee and David ride in it while I pull. Like I said, they're a little spoiled, but it's not too bad, and besides, I don't want to start off pulling rank on them too much. I want them to get used to me first.

Of course the minute we get in sight of the dock they want ice cream. So we stop in for that delicious ice cream, and gross!—there's Barry working behind the counter. What's he doing here? He turns red like a beet when he sees me. I'm really surprised to see him working. I thought that all rich kids ever do is go boating and play tennis.

"Hi," I say and give him one of my nicest smiles. I still feel pretty bad about what I did say to him on the pier. I guess I always will. "I didn't know you were working here."

"Only part time," he says, "three afternoons a week." And then he says hi to the kids and gives them a nice smile. He barely looks at me and starts concentrating on the vanilla ice cream.

"I want the jumbo double scoop!" David says.

"Me too! Me too!" DeeDee starts jumping up and down.

"Uh-uh," I say. "I don't have that kind of money. Besides, I didn't even ask your mother if you could have ice cream anyhow."

"Mommy always buys us a double scoop after lunch, right, DeeDee?" David says, pushing DeeDee.

"Yeah, always," she says right on cue. I know they're both full of it, but they're making such a fuss I figure I'll treat them, so I say okay.

Barry starts to scoop the ice cream and they keep changing flavors so they end up with almost four different scoops apiece. He only charges me for singles anyway.

"How do you like it so far?" he asks me, and I can see he's not so angry anymore.

"Pretty good," I tell him. "I really like it."

"Where are you?"

"Over on Evergreen."

"Yeah? I know where that is."

"Right after Seaview," I say.

"There's a yellow house with turrets on the corner."

"Right," I say. "That's practically across the street from us. We're in the white house with the red shutters."

"Yeah, I think I know it."

That's it. Now we have nothing in the whole world to say. Maybe I should start the geography lesson again.

"Would you like to get together sometime?" he finally says. "We could play tennis—just as friends, I mean."

I wince at that.

"Do you play tennis?" he asks.

"A little."

"Well, we could play a couple of sets . . . or there's this disco where a lot of kids hang out . . . we could go there."

"Sure, that would be nice."

"Should I call you?"

"Sure." What else can I say? I mean, he's being so nice and friendly, especially after the embarrassing time yesterday.

I give him my number and tell him thanks for the extra ice cream and head off in the direction of Cherry Grove.

Fire Island is great. You can never get lost. All it is is a long skinny strip of sand off the coast of Long Island. The Atlantic Ocean is on one side and the bay is on the other. If the Dunes restaurant is on the way to Cherry Grove, there's no way you can miss it. You just keep walking and you have to hit it. The kids aren't too hot to go but I make a deal with them. It's really very simple—they sit in the wagon and I pull. By the time the summer ends they'll probably forget how to walk and I'll have gorilla arms.

The Dunes is a big outdoor-indoor restaurant right on the beach. It's busy and there are a lot of people sitting around eating. There are some women and a few kids, but mostly there are men. I already know that Cherry Grove is a big gay hangout. These two guys, friends of my parents, have been coming out here every summer for years and my parents always spend a weekend with them. Naturally my folks are planning to come out this summer, and I'm not looking forward to that. I'm sort of a different person out here already. It's like this is kind of my place and being somebody's little girl out here is going to bug me. I just know it. Well, I've got a good four weeks, before my parents come, to worry about it. Anyway, I look around but I don't see Jim, but of course he could be inside, so I tell the kids not to move and I go inside to see if I can find him. He's there. The first waiter I see.

I work my way around to his table and come up from behind and tap him on the shoulder.

"Hi," I say, and I can't believe I'm doing it. I mean

this is so unlike me. Mostly I plan things for a hundred years in advance, and then at the last minute I lose my courage and think of a million reasons why I can't do it.

"Hey," he says, turning around. "How you doing?" And I can see he's surprised to see me. But he gives me such a nice smile that my knees begin to wobble.

"Okay. You working here?"

"Right, uh . . . er . . ."

"Victoria." I don't know why I did that. I'm sure he knows my name.

"Sure, Victoria, I didn't forget." See, I told you. "How's Barry?"

"Gee, I don't know. I haven't seen him in ages," I lie.

"We played tennis this morning."

"Yeah, he told me." Oh, damn. ". . . Ages ago."

Jim kind of chuckles and so do I, and then I ask him what's to do here and where do the kids hang out and he says mostly at night everyone goes to The Monkey, a disco.

I tell him that I have Monday nights off and maybe I'll drop by The Monkey. "Will you be there this Monday?" I ask as offhandedly as you can possibly be asking someone for a date.

"Probably," he says, and I manage to say, "Maybe I'll see you there." And then he says he has to go, and I say, "See you later," and he says, "See you later," and I'm so excited I almost walk into the wall.

I can't believe I did it. I actually did it. I got to see Jim and practically have a date with him. And I did it all by myself. He didn't even help.

I'm flying. The kids are outside, right where I left them, driving some old lady crazy. They're saying curse words back and forth to each other and going hysterical, and the lady keeps saying how that's not nice and nice children don't talk like that and on and on, and the more she tells them not to, the dirtier they talk, and it's so embarrassing I don't even want to go over and get them.

"DeeDee!" I call from a pretty safe distance. "David! C'mon."

But they're having too good a time freaking the lady out, so I have to go over and practically drag them to the wagon. David is smart enough to keep his mouth shut, but DeeDee lets fly with one last zonker that nearly knocks the poor lady off her seat. It is a little too much for a five-year-old.

I pile them both in the wagon and zoom off along the beach. Now you have to appreciate something that I didn't understand until I got to Fire Island. You know, a lot of people don't wear bathing suits on the beach. But nobody told me, so here I am walking along the beach pulling these two deadweights and at first I'm not even looking around, I'm just pulling with my head down and my mind on Jim, then I catch a look at this guy and I'm past him befire I realize he's naked and I stop dead (really cool huh?) and slowly sneak a look. And my jaw drops. Almost everyone is naked, guys and girls, and because there's no one else there I have to say it to David and DeeDee. "Look at those people."

And they look and then David says, "What about them?"

"Are you kidding? They're naked, that's what's about them."

"Victoria?" Now David's going to ask me about them, and I don't know what to say. I hope he doesn't ask me something physical, because now that I'm looking around I don't think I want to go into the whole anatomy thing.

"Can we go swimming now?" Huh? Unreal! He doesn't even care. It has to be because they've been coming out here all their lives and naked human beings are common sights to them. Completely natural. Well, let me tell you, *I'm* freaking out. I'm trying to be cool, but, wow, will you look at all those penises! Crazy thought: Do my parents go naked when they come out here? I'm so busy watching and planning what I'm going to write to Steffi that I run us, wagon and all, into the water four times.

The closer you get to Ocean Beach the more crowded the beach gets and the fewer naked people you see, and by the time we're in the middle of Ocean Beach there's only one or two and they're girls and only topless. I wish Steffi was here.

We swim for a while and get back to the house by four. Cynthia is out on the deck sunning herself. I guess she's feeling better.

I get up to my room and it's boiling hot. I think DeeDee must be wrong, that it would be too hot for a closet. I guess it's terrific in the winter. There's a whole pile of DeeDee's dresses and a couple of David's things on my bed with a note from Cynthia that says if I wouldn't mind pressing these clothes when I got a chance she'd really appreciate it.

I roll up the laundry because I'm too exhausted to do it today, but it's a problem finding a space to store it. I told you it's a very cozy room and there's not a whole lot of extra space. I end up putting it on the corner of my bed with my tennis racket and my blow dryer.

Dinner is super. Cynthia is a fantastic cook. She does something to the hamburgers with Worcestershire sauce and butter and herbs that's the best I ever had. She says it's from Craig Claiborne or somebody. She's sort of a gourmet cook. I'm really lucky because I love the way she cooks.

"Listen, Victoria," she says to me over dinner, "please don't rush with that ironing. It doesn't have to be done tonight. Just do as much as you feel like and you can finish the rest at your leisure." Then Cynthia says she has to go get dressed. She's a little excited because she has a date with this man she met last night at The Dunes.

"That's all right," I say. "I don't mind ironing. Besides, I hate to just sit and watch TV. I like to be doing something." That's not exactly true, but I want her to see that I'm not lazy like last year's mother's helper, who, she keeps telling me, was practically comatose.

I'm a lousy ironer, so it takes me until almost one o'clock in the morning to finish all the stuff, and I'm dripping wet when I do so I take a shower and practically fall into bed.

Then I remember that I absolutely have to write Steffi tonight if I want her to get the letter before she leaves for her camping trip. Besides, I have a million crucial things to tell her, except that when I actually write the letter it takes me two full pages of really tiny writing to get through the part about work. I'm too exhausted to even start about Jim, so I just stuff what I wrote into an envelope, turn out the light, and dive into the bed.

Suddenly I'm wide awake. What if what Gloria said was right? Is this a terrible job? Is Cynthia taking advantage? But she's not. I just know it. Cynthia's very nice in a lot of ways, even though I can't think of exactly what ones they are this very minute. Maybe this is what it's really like being a mother's helper. Not that I do all that much. Still, it's sort of more than I expected—maybe because it's new and I don't have the hang of it yet.

Boy, if my mother knew all the work I was doing, she'd faint.

9

It can't be morning yet. It can't be. But it is because DeeDee is climbing all over me, pulling at the
covers and telling me she's hungry. I try to tell her
that she's big enough to take a glass of juice for herself
and watch TV until I get downstairs. But she says she
can't squeeze the juice herself and I remember that
Cynthia likes to have freshly squeezed orange juice in
the morning.

"How about a glass of milk instead?" I ask her.

"You said juice."

"Milk's better."

"I want juice."

There's no way. Once DeeDee makes up her mind,
that's it. So I drag myself out of bed and go downstairs
and fix her breakfast, which she leaves over half of,
anyway. I turn on the TV and curl up on the couch
and try to sleep a little more. No luck. David's heard
us, and now he wants breakfast, too. I think maybe
these kids could do a little more for themselves, but I
guess that's up to the mother.

There's the cutest note from Cynthia that says how
she had a great time and she got in late so we should
go to the beach without her. It's written like a please-
excuse-Cynthia note from school. See, that's one of the
nice things about her, she's got a terrific sense of humor.

We do the beach bit again, and today there are a
few more people on the beach. I guess it's beginning to

fill up for the Fourth of July weekend. There are some other mother's helpers with kids, and we all kind of sit close by and the kids begin to play together, and then we start to talk and a couple of them are nice girls and we'll probably get friendly.

One girl, Dana, is tall, with a great figure and legs that look like they go on forever. She's got long hair, sort of light brown with blond streaks, and the nicest smile. I know I'm going to like her, and besides, she's new like me. She takes care of two kids too, but one is a two-year-old baby and the other is a five-year-old girl like DeeDee. In fact, Leah—that's the kid's name—and DeeDee get along fine together.

The other mother's helper if from last year, and her name is Anita. She has reddish-brown hair so short and curly that it almost looks kinky, and she's so cute and little she could pass for fifteen but she's actually seventeen. She's got only one kid and he's almost eight, so she really has it easy, and besides, she says, they have other help in the house so she doesn't have to do anything but take care of Scott. And she says she gets forty dollars a week. Even Dana gets more than me. Not that much—thirty dollars—but still . . . it's okay with me because I know Cynthia's not being cheap. Not deliberately, anyway. She just can't afford to pay me any more.

"I knew the girl who worked for the Landrys last year," Anita says. "And she says Mr. Landry was always trying to flirt with her. Can you imagine trying to make out with your own mother's helper? Isn't that disgusting?"

Ugh, we all say. "I 'm really glad he isn't around," I tell them.

Anita goes on.

"And she said Mrs. Landry wasn't so great either. She didn't do a whole lot."

"I heard about that girl last year," I say. "Her name was Christie, right?"

"Yeah," Anita says.

"Cynthia—that's Mrs. Landry," I say, "she said that Christie was really lazy with a capital L. All she wanted to do was sit around and polish her nails."

"That's all I want to do too," Dana says, and we all laugh because she's right.

Then we all compare our jobs, and it turns out that mine is the worst. Far and away. But I don't let them see how bad it really is because I'm sort of embarrassed. Besides, it's not as though Cynthia is mean or anything like that—in fact she's probably a lot nicer than the woman Anita works for, who sounds like a real bitch. The trouble with Cynthia is that she's used to having a housekeeper, so it's just natural for her to leave the work to someone else, and besides she's probably very depressed and not herself because of the divorce and all her troubles.

Then there's something else. I'm really sort of stuck. I don't want to just quit because then I'd have to leave Fire Island and Jim, and also it'd be like admitting to my parents that I just can't hack it. And of course I'd have to tell Cynthia, and I don't think I'd have the nerve unless she really did something awful to me. In the meantime I'm just going to let things go the way they are and keep my eyes open in case something else comes up. According to Anita, after two weeks all the mothers hate their helpers and all the helpers are ready to switch. I think I'll just wait and see.

"I don't care how much she makes me work, I really like Cynthia," I tell Anita and Dana, and I find myself feeling bad because I don't want people not to like the person I'm working for. It's just that she's having a hard time now, and I tell them what a bastard Jed was.

"Cynthia's really pretty," Anita says, and we decide that she's one of the best-looking mothers around. And I don't know why, but that makes me feel good. We're on the beach for three hours, and Dana and I sit there listening to the stories Anita tells us. She knows all the juice and there's enough dirt to bury the whole island. The stories are all about adultery. It's like nobody's happily married. Always when I hear all these stories I go home and worry about my own parents. Except that's impossible. I just can't picture my mother fooling around. And my father! I practically break up trying to picture that. Listen, I have enough trouble thinking about them making it together.

We rotate lying in the sun. One of us watches the kids while the other two get a tan. Dana is on watch now.

"Gorgeous!" Dana says. "Absolutely knockout stuff." Anita and I pop right up. Gorgeous can only mean a guy.

"Where?" Anita says, grabbing for her sunglasses. They're prescription glasses and she's practically blind without them. But she pretends they're only sunglasses.

"There," Dana says, pointing to two surfers right in front of us in the water. It takes me two seconds to realize they're Jim and Barry.

"They're both cute," Anita says, "but the blond is sensational."

Naturally she's talking about my Jim. He really does look like an advertisement.

"I know them," I say as casually as I can. And they both nearly jump out of their skins. They have a million questions, and I can tell from the questions, that Dana really digs Barry, which sort of surprises me a little. I don't tell how Barry feels about me.

We watch the guys surfing, and it's funny but they're both a lot like the way they surf. I mean their personalities. Barry's pretty good, but he doesn't seem to take it too seriously. He looks as if he's having a lot of fun. Even when he falls off he seems to be laughing. Another thing: he's so busy surfing that he doesn't

seem to be aware of the people on the beach. He's just
having a great old time.

But Jim knows he's got an audience (I guess someone who looks the way he does always has an audience) and he's playing to them. I don't mean he's not
having fun, but you can tell by the way he stands on
the surfboard that he wants to look his best. And boy,
he sure does. Dana's right. He's gorgeous. And he's a
very good surfer, too, his blond hair whipping back,
his arms straight out as though he's flying, and a big
happy smile on his face. I wish he really was my boyfriend. I'd love that more than anything else in the
world. And I'd love everyone to know.

Suddenly it seems that all the mother's helpers who
normally detest the water are nagging their charges to
go in. Me too. Except I don't have to ask twice because
David is always ready. Even DeeDee wants to go in.

Like lemmings we all head toward the water.
Counting the kids, we must be about fifteen. There
are so many of us bobbing in the water that if the guys
still want to do serious surfing they'll have to move
farther down the beach. I guess the temptation of all
those cute girl lemmings is just too much, because
pretty soon we're all fooling around on their surf-
boards and nobody's taking anything seriously. Except
dumb me, I always take Jim seriously. Kind of cuts
into my fun but I can't help it. That's just the way I
feel about him.

Jim shows David how to hold on to the board and I
feel super because he picked my kid. That must mean
something.

By the time we finish with the water and head up to
our blankets Jim has a group of female admirers
around him you wouldn't believe. Actually it's disgusting, except he doesn't seem to think so. In fact, he
looks like he can hardly tear himself away. When I see
how popular he is it makes me think I'm probably
wasting my time. I'll never get him.

Out of the corner of my eye I see Dana talking to Barry. I told you she liked him. And he seems kind of interested in her, which is a little annoying, particularly since he's supposed to be so crazy about me. Not that I really care because he definitely isn't my type. It's just that he made such a big thing about how he felt about me. Sometimes guys really give me a pain.

"Hey, buddy," Jim calls to Barry, "I gotta get back. Are you coming?"

"Sure thing," Barry says and grabs his board.

"See you around," Jim says, and he gives everybody one of his big heart-stopping smiles. Then he sort of points at me and says, "At The Monkey, right?" And I nearly drop dead.

"Take it easy." Barry waves, and they both go off down the beach.

The other girls drift off to their own blankets, and I just stand there staring.

"Wake up," Anita says.

"Did he point at me or did he point at me, huh?" I ask them both, and I'm positively freaking out.

"He definitely pointed at you," Dana says.

And then I ask them about six more times if they're absolutely certain it was at me, and they swear it was, and I still can hardly believe it. I would go on about it for another half hour except that Dana has a million questions about Barry that I have to answer. Like I said, she's interested in him. I tell her everything I know about him except how he feels about me, which he probably doesn't anymore anyway.

"Are you going to The Monkey later?" Anita asks me as we break up and head back to our houses.

"Are you kidding?" I say. "There's no way I'm not going to be there tonight."

"See you later then." They both wave and go off.

10

We're pretty late getting back for lunch. Cynthia probably couldn't wait for us so she left a note saying she went to the Youngs' for lunch and would I pretty please make the kids tuna sandwiches and see if I can't sort of straighten out the house a little because some friends are coming for cocktails. P.S., she says, the vacuum is in the pantry closet, and so is the mop. Goodbye afternoon for me.

But I don't mind because if she's having company, it means she'll be home tonight and I can get out for sure. Fantastic!

After lunch David goes to his friends across the street and DeeDee is so tired from the beach she takes a nap. Lucky for me, because it's going to take me a while to get things in shape. There's another note from Cynthia on the kitchen table that says only to change her sheets, everyone else's is clean. I start on the downstairs first so I can be sure that's ready for the company. I'm just starting to drag the vacuum up the steps when the phone rings. At first I leap for it, but then I remember about the grandfather and I just stand there and let it ring. But—I know this a long shot—but maybe it's Jim. Maybe he asked Barry for my number and . . . No way. Still . . . I answer it.

"Hello?" Very sweet, warm, intelligent person of at least sixteen. That's me.

"Cynthia?"

"No, she's not home. This is the mother's helper."

"Mother's what?"

"The mother's helper. You know, I take care of the kids and . . ."

"Great little kids, aren't they?" whoever he is says, cutting me off right in the middle of my sentence. "Best in the world. How about putting David on?"

"David's not home. Who is this, please?"

"What about DeeDee?" he says without answering my question. Except I think I know the answer already. "Isn't she home?"

"She's sleeping," I say. "Is this Mr. Landry?"

"How'd you know?" And he gets a suspicious tone to his voice.

"Cynthia said that you might call."

"What'd she tell you?"

Now I'm his enemy and that makes me start to fumffer all over the place.

"Nothing . . . except she said . . . uh . . . she thought it would be better if you didn't . . . I mean . . . she said . . ."

"She don't want me to talk to the kids, right?"

"Well . . ." Even though he's not exactly sweet and gentle the way I expected, still it's hard to tell him he can't talk to his own grandchildren. And he seems to be reading my thoughts. He says, "Look, honey, those kids are my flesh and blood—she ain't got no right to do this."

"I'm sorry, Mr. Landry, but I'm only the mother's helper."

"Well, listen here, mother's helper or whatever you are, you get that little girl awake and let her talk to her grandpa. You hear me?"

This is terrible. Cynthia said I should hang up, but I can't slam the phone down on someone I practically know, especially a grandfather. "Please, Mr. Landry, can you call back when Cynthia is here?"

"That won't do me no good, that girl's too sour. I ain't saying she's wrong about that boy—a rotten kid

Jed is sometimes—but she ain't got no right doing this to me and the kids. I'm their grandpa and we got a right to be together. You got a grandpa?"

"Yes, sir."

"You love him?"

"Oh, yes, definitely. I love him very much."

"What'd you think somebody steps in there and says you can't see him and they've got no good reason?"

"Cynthia thinks maybe you could talk to your son about the money."

"I talked to him about that more'n she has. He's just a downright nasty boy and I'm ashamed of him. If I had a penny more on my Social Security, I'd pay it myself."

Now I feel even worse. I mean, the poor man has no money. I think maybe Cynthia is wrong about doing it this way. But what can I do?

"Please, Mr. Landry, I don't know what to do. I have to do what Cynthia told me. Maybe you could call when she's home."

"No good. Tell you what, just wake DeeDee up and let me talk to her."

"I can't, Mr. Landry. Please don't ask me to do something like that."

"But you know it ain't right what she's doing. I'm an old man . . . uh, what'd you say your name was?"

"Victoria."

"Victoria, you sound like a nice girl. Let me tell you. I ain't so young anymore and maybe I don't have too much time left. I don't mean I'm sick or anything, but I'm past seventy and . . . tell you the truth, honey, those kids is all I have. And I'm the only grandpa they have and . . . well, there ain't much in my life I'm so crazy about, but those kids, they're special. I guess I love them more than I do . . . well, anyone."

When I hear his voice break I start to fall apart myself. Nobody has ever talked to me like that before. I mean I never had the power to say yes or no like this. It's terrible. I hate it.

Right in the middle of everything DeeDee comes down from her nap, still half asleep and creeps onto my lap and snuggles up. She's soft and all warm from sleep and so lovable.

"Who's that you're talking to," she asks, and I cover the phone. But it's too late.

"That DeeDee?" Mr. Landry asks in a loud voice, and suddenly he sounds so excited. "DeeDee, it's Grandpa!"

Well, forget it. I'm not going to do something I know is really wrong just because someone tells me to. And in a giant burst of—I don't know, maybe courage or maybe the opposite, maybe I'm too weak to stand up—I put the phone up to DeeDee's ear.

And her face lights up. "Grandpa!" And then to me, "It's my grandpa!" And then back to the phone. "Grandpa, I told Victoria all about you and we saw a fisherman today and he wasn't half as good as you, and I told him how my grandpa is the best fisherman in the whole world and David said so too. . . . I miss you too. . . . When are you coming out to see us? . . . How come? I want you to come today . . . I want you to come tomorrow then." And then she turns to me and says, "My grandpa can't come out this week, that's what he said. . . . How come, Grandpa?" She's back talking into the phone and they go on for a while, and she's so cute, and she tells him all about every single thing that happened since she came out here. I mean everything, like what she ate for breakfast, and he asks her lots of questions, and you can tell he's really interested in everything about her. And then they say, "I love you," and they throw kisses and finally they say good-bye and the call probably cost him a fortune. I know people get very little money on Social Security so I guess he'll have to do without something else to make up for talking to his granddaughter. I'm in a lot of trouble so I'm building up his case. First thing I have to make sure is that DeeDee doesn't say anything to Cynthia.

"You really have a terrific grandpa, DeeDee," I start off.

And she loves that and she tells me all the things they talked about on the phone, which of course I just heard.

"Do you have any special secrets with your grandpa?"

"What's a special secret?"

"Something you have that nobody else in the whole world knows. I have one with my grandpa."

"What about?"

"I can't tell you. Then it wouldn't be my special secret."

"I want one too." And she wants one so much she's beginning to pout. So I give her one.

"Okay, DeeDee, that phone call from your grandpa, the one just now, that's you special secret. Now, remember, don't tell anyone else."

" 'Cept my mommy. But not David."

"Not even your mommy if you want it to be a special secret." I feel so low tricking a baby like this.

"Not even my mommy?"

"Right. Not even your mommy. And you know what happens to people who keep their special grandpa secrets at the end of the summer?"

"Uh-uh." And her eyes get twice their size. These kids can smell a prize a mile away.

"They get a prize."

"A kangaroo?"

"Maybe so."

"Ooooh." And she jumps up and down and claps her hands.

"Are you going to keep the special grandpa secret?"

She thinks hard for a minute and says, "I'll ask my mommy."

I try a different approach. "DeeDee, if you tell your mommy about your grandpa calling, my grandpa is going to be very upset and I will be too because then you won't be a member of the Secret Grandpa Club and then you won't be able to come to the meetings or get the button or anything." I can see I'm getting to her. She's a little confused but the button's got to get her.

"I want the button," she finally announces. What did I tell you?

"Then don't tell Mommy."

"Let me see it."

"If you don't tell Mommy."

"Okay."

"My grandpa is going to be verry happy, and me too."

"Victoria?"

"What, sweetie?"

"I want my button."

"I'm going to write away this very afternoon."

"I want it now." And she screws her face up like she's going to cry.

"I have to write away, DeeDee. Look, I don't even have mine yet."

"You promised."

"I know and I'm going to do it right now. See?" And I take a scrap of paper and start to write some gibberish.

"Maybe if I ask my mommy she can call on the phone and then they can bring it over today."

"They don't have any phones and besides if you tell your mommy anything, all the buttons will turn green and melt away." She's pushing me. If it was Nina I'd tell her *she'd* turn green and melt away. It's so much easier with a sister.

"I swear I won't tell, ever, ever. . . ."

"That's fine. Now let's finish cleaning up for the company."

"Send the letter." She says it like a midget general. Now that I've created a button monster, I'm not about to screw up so I put the letter in an envelope and tell her I'm sending it special delivery. That sounds okay to her and we—well, not exactly we, more like I— finish cleaning. I hope I do a good enough job because I never really cleaned a whole house like this. At home the most I do is some dishes, and when they really bug me enough, my own room. I finish just before Cynthia comes home and am I pooped. Cynthia says I did a terrific job. She tells me to start dinner for the kids while she throws herself together for her company.

While she's talking to me, DeeDee is whispering in my ear how I should ask Cynthia if I can go to the post office. The kid's developed a button fixation. I don't know if this is going to work.

"DeeDee, DeeDee darling," Cynthia says, "what's all the whispering about?"

Before DeeDee can open her mouth, I jump in with how we have a special secret. I do a lot of winking and smiling at Cynthia and make her promise not to ask us any more. Of course, she goes right along with it, and in that adult-pretended-interest way she says, "It's wonderful," and starts upstairs.

"And I'm gonna get a button too, right, Victoria?" DeeDee, the button maniac, says.

"That's terrific," Cynthia says, and disappears up the stairs. So far so good. It's horrendous having your entire career in the hands of a five-year-old.

Cynthia's company comes at five, and it turns out to be Eva and Ron Thompson, the people Anita works for. Anita told a whole juicy adultery story about them, and I can't keep from gaping at them, especially her. After they have a couple of drinks (this is going to blow your mind) I think I see Cynthia and Ron Thompson giving each other little special looks. Wow! This is a weird place.

I feed the kids and it's almost seven and Cynthia

and her guests are still having cocktails. Now another couple from down the street comes over, and it's sort of turning into a party and Cynthia looks hot to get rid of me. So she says when I put the kids in bed I can go out for a while. Super!

I dive into my makeup. I don't need too much because I'm really getting a great tan, but I do my eyes and put on my fabulous new lipliner with the pale gloss on the inside. A final touch or two and down I go.

Cynthia is so involved that she doesn't even see me come downstairs, but I don't want to leave without letting her know so I sort of stand around waiting to catch her attention. Finally she sees me so I give her a little wave and start out the door.

"Victoria, honey," Cynthia calls me, "wait a sec, will you?"

I stop at the door.

"Honey," she says, coming over to me, "I hate to do this to you, but I think there's been a change in plans and we might go over to the Thompsons' later for some drinks so I don't think you'd better go out."

"But I told some people. . . ." One look at her face and I know it's no use.

"I'm really sorry, dear, but . . . maybe tomorrow. Tomorrow night for sure."

There's nothing I can really say. I mean, she's paying me to take care of the kids, and if she decides to go out I can't tell her not to. Still, that seems sort of mean because she isn't even sure if she really is going. She only said they might. Maybe they're not planning to go for a couple of hours. I wouldn't care if I could only stay for a little while.

"If you're not going for a while," I say, "I could be back in an hour, even less."

"No, dear, I don't like to be tied down. Come on, Victoria, don't look so unhappy, you have a whole summer ahead of you."

That's the same garbage I told David. There's no point in standing there with my face hanging out so I go back upstairs and I cry.

Well, that's not so peculiar considering I'm very disappointed, and besides this was practically a semidate with Jim and now it's going to be like I'm standing him up and that's certainly going to be the end for me. Can you picture anyone standing Jim up and getting another chance? Never.

There's got to be a way to get out tonight.

11

I must have fallen asleep because next thing I know it's midnight and the house is quiet. I'm still dressed so I slip out of bed and creep downstairs to see what's up.

The living room is empty so they must have all gone out. I check on the kids and they're sleeping fine. Cynthia's door is open so I go in to get the new *Vogue* she said I could borrow. I'm not in the least tired. Just miserable.

I'm two steps into the room when I see Cynthia is in her bed sleeping. She didn't go out after all.

Damn. I could have gone. She really stinks. Maybe she came up to tell me and saw me sleeping and figured I wouldn't want to go. Still, she could have waked me and asked. She must have seen I was dressed. I think she's kind of selfish. She probably didn't even think about me at all. Maybe I'm not so crazy about her anymore. If I tried hard enough I could probably hate her guts. She ruined my entire summer. Maybe my entire life. Damn her!

Maybe I should wake her up and ask her if I could go now. Ten after twelve isn't that late for a disco. Nah.

She'd probably say it's too late to be going out. "What would your mother say?" or something like that. Besides, I wouldn't have the nerve to wake her up just to ask her if I could go out dancing. Even if it is just possibly the most important night of my life.

I'll never be able to sleep tonight. I just know it.

There's no way . . . unless. I know this probably
sounds really sneaky but suppose I just went out without saying anything. It's not like I'm not doing my
job, because Cynthia's home and the kids are sleeping
and everything is under control. I could go for just a
little while and be back and nobody would know the
difference.

I'm not saying it's the best thing in the world to do,
but it certainly isn't going to hurt anyone except me if
I don't do it.

If I keep analyzing it I'll never do it. So I stop analyzing, fix my hair, put on more gloss, and tiptoe
down the steps like a thief, feeling awful. The house is
deadly quiet. I turn the door latch as delicately as I
can so there'll be no thunderous click to wake the
house up. It works. I'd probably make a great burglar.
Anyway, I'm out and my heart is pounding.

12

I don't have any trouble finding The Monkey. Half-way down to the dock, I can hear the music. It's almost twelve-thirty, but the place is packed and the overflow is hanging out all over the front steps and into the street. Mostly everyone is wearing jean shorts and T-shirts, which is perfect. At least I guessed right, and I love my top—it's sort of a camisole with laces up the front. Very sexy. Last time I wore it my father made me put on a shirt underneath. But that's the great thing about being out here. I'm on my own, and I think it looks just fine without anything underneath.

I kind of hang back a little—maybe I'll see someone I know. I hope not Barry.

"Vicky! Hey, over here!" It's Dana. Great!

"Hi!" I call, and head toward her.

"I figured you weren't going to show. What happened?" she says.

"Cynthia took forever to decide she wasn't going out."

I look inside at the people. There must be a hundred of them all jammed together, drinking and laughing and dancing on the tiny dance floor. "Boy, this is wild," I exclaim.

"Is this your first time here?"

"Yeah. It looks great."

"C'mon, let's go in."

The music bombs your ears and the lights spin around so fast that you couldn't tell if your own sister was here. Boy, what a thought. It's hopeless to try to find Jim until the lights slow up. Somebody taps me on the shoulder, and when I turn around it's some guy I don't know. He makes a "dance?" sign. No point in talking—you can't hear a thing anyway. I nod yes and we squeeze our way onto the dance floor.

Like I told you, I'm a pretty good dancer. It's the one time I feel I've got it all together—when I'm dancing, I mean. I wish I could feel this way all the time.

The next record is Joni Mitchell singing "Court and Spark." She really blows my mind. Now, before I can make my way to Dana, some other guy asks me to dance. He's kind of cute but too tall for me. I hate to slow-dance with a real tall guy. It's so boring to stare into the middle of a T-shirt.

The lights slow down and I find Dana. She's with Anita.

"I heard my people were at your house," she says. "What do you think of them?"

"She's gross, but he's kind of cute in a goopy sort of sweet way."

"Right," she says.

"This is going to blow your mind," I tell her, "but I think Cynthia has the hots for your boss's husband."

"Ron? You have to be kidding! He's so . . . like shy."

"That's what you think. You should see him come on to Cynthia."

"Good. I hope so. She deserves it—Eva, I mean. You know what she did to him tonight? She . . ." But the music starts blasting and you can't hear. A guy asks Anita to dance, and then someone puts his hand on my shoulder, and when I turn around my knees almost crumble.

"Victoria?" It's *him*. He smiles at me and motions to dance. I don't even look around at Dana. I'll apologize later. I just follow him through the crowd onto the dance floor.

I can't believe he's asked me to dance. And it turns out he's a great dancer and it's like we've been dancing together forever—I mean, we just groove so good. I can tell he knows it too. We can't talk because of the music, but we dance the next two dances even though someone else comes up and asks me. He shakes his head no to the guy, and I do too.

Three dances practically wipe us out, and he takes my arm and leads me toward the door. I'm soaking wet. And more excited than I've ever been in my life. I'm so knocked out at the thought that I'm with Jim that I can hardly catch my breath, and that's not just from dancing either.

We get outside and he keeps going past the kids hanging on the steps and toward the dock. I think I would follow him anywhere. Just the feel of his hand on my arm makes me tingle. We don't talk until we get to the end of the dock, and then he stops.

"Want to sit here for a while and just cool off?" he asks, sitting down on the edge of the pier and making room for me.

I should say, "Yes, good idea," and sit next to him, but all I can manage in my freaked-out condition is a smile as I sit down.

He takes a joint out of his shirt pocket and lights up. Then he takes a couple of drags to get it going and hands it to me.

I'm not a big grass smoker. For one thing, my parents are always warning me how it's illegal and if you get caught terrible things can happen to you. And for another, I don't trust it. Sometimes I get feeling really cool and great, but most of the time I get nutty giddy and absolutely anything breaks me up. Other times I just sit there and cough my head off. I really don't feel like doing the ten-minute cough number tonight, so, just not to take any chances, I barely inhale any. Also, it's tough enough for me to handle what's happening straight. But stoned? Forget it.

"You're a sensational dancer," he says to me, and he turns and looks down at me with just a little bit of a tiny smile. I smile a thank-you, and it's funny but we both keep looking at each other and wow!—it feels to me like we're almost touching.

"And you're pretty too," he says.

This time I manage a thank-you and even more.

"You're a good dancer too," I tell him.

"And am I pretty too?" he says, smiling his usual beautiful up-the-corner smile with white even teeth that you can see into. He flips the end of the joint into the water, then very gently he brushes a straggly strand of hair out of my eyes. And the smile gets smaller and more private, and we sit there silently looking at each other, and I don't even feel that we have to talk. He moves closer and his thigh brushes against mine, and the feel of this touch zings through my body and makes me shiver a tiny bit.

"Cold?" he asks.

"A little," I lie, because how else can I explain the shiver? He puts his arm around my shoulder and gently pulls me closer to him. My head is against his chest and he feels warm and I can hear his heart beating. It's going pretty fast. I think mine must be too. I'm staring down at the water, but all I can think of is should I say something or should I just sit here and let him hold me like this. I only practically just met him. I mean, this is the first time I've ever been with him alone like this. While I'm in the middle of the big decision, he says my name, softly, and when I look up to answer him, he kisses me.

His lips are unbelievably soft, and as he bends down to me he pulls me up toward him. And what starts off as a light kiss grows stronger and harder until our lips are pressed against our teeth and I feel his mouth begin to open and I pull back a tiny bit, not far, but enough so that he sees that I don't want him to do that. Still kissing me, he leans back on the dock and pulls me down with him. Anyone else tried this the first time and I would just push him away, but I don't move. The tops of our bodies are tight against each other but the bottoms are still facing the way we were when we were sitting. Now Jim rolls over toward me and with one arm pulls me close to him. I don't even pull away. It's like I'm not inside myself. All I want to do is be near him.

He takes his lips off mine and lifts his head and leans on one elbow. His face is only inches away from mine and he looks very serious.

"Is something wrong?" he asks me, really concerned. I must look scared because I am, a little.

"Uh-uh." I shake my head. "It's just that . . . I don't know. I guess I didn't expect this. . . . I guess."

"Me neither," and he smiles and I think he's got the most trusting face I ever saw.

He kisses me again, and this time I feel more relaxed, like I know him better. I'm feeling really happy and good, and then I begin to get sort of lost in the kiss, in his closeness, and when his mouth opens against mine I let mine open too. He puts his tongue against my teeth and I don't know what's the matter with me, I never kiss this way with anyone. But I do with Jim, and then I even let him put his tongue inside my mouth and his hand runs down the side of my body, sort of over my hip and down the side of my leg and I don't do anything. I mean I don't stop him and I don't even want to.

The way he touches me doesn't feel like other guys who just want to grab you: it's like he's caressing me and it makes me want to caress him but of course I don't. No matter what, I don't think I ever could. My eyes are always closed when I kiss, but now I open them a tiny bit just because I have to look at him. His eyes are closed, shut tight, and he's got blond eyelashes. I didn't know that. Suddenly I become tense because the hand that was caressing my side is moving up under my arm and I'm afraid he's going to try to touch my breast. Besides, I'm very ticklish. He feels me jump a little and his hand moves away, down my side again, and he pulls me closer and moves his face down to kiss my neck and that makes me really shiver. Nice shiver. I know this is too much but I can't stop it. I can, but I don't want to. It's the first time in my whole life I ever felt like this.

Now he brings his lips back to mine and we're kissing and I'm kissing just as hard as he is and my arms are around his back and I'm holding him tight and I feel like I don't care what happens.

His hand comes up under my arm again and he lets it brush lightly over my breasts, and my head is buzzing but I don't even stop him, and now his hand covers my whole breast and I can't think of anything else except what he's doing and that I'm letting him. How could I let him do this? What's the matter with me?

The awful thing is that it feels good. I won't let him go any further, and I'm beginning to tense up waiting for him to try. But he doesn't and I kind of let myself relax and he kisses me and I kiss him and our whole bodies are tight together and I'll worry about everything later.

We kiss like this for a long while, and then I feel him push his legs into mine and I feel a hardness against my thigh and I know it isn't his keys and I feel kind of scared because maybe this is getting out of control. Maybe I won't be able to stop him. But I can because it's Jim and I know him, and besides, everyone says he's a terrific guy and he would never do anything like push himself on someone who didn't want him to. He's not like that, I just know it. But still I feel a little scared, so I pull back slightly and he pushes against me kind of hard, and I open my eyes and pull my face away from his, and he looks at me and sort of swallows hard and takes a couple of

breaths and gives me an it's-all-right smile and goes
back to gently kissing me.

But it doesn't stay that way long and we're back to
holding each other tightly, and now his hand is working around my camisole straps and I should have worn
the damned T-shirt underneath like my father said.
Oh, God, what a time to think of my father. That does
it. I push his hand away and he puts it back the minute I push it away.

"Please . . ." I say, "don't do that."

He moves his hand away from my straps and slides
it down the side of my leg to the top of my thigh. Now
I really push it away.

"Please . . ." I say again, and he starts to kiss my
neck and my ear, and then his hand is on my breast
again, but I already let him do that so I can't say no
now. Besides, that's not so bad, I think. Sometimes his
hand slips off the material and onto my bare skin and I
get goose bumps. It slips off more and more and I
know he's trying to put his hand under my camisole
and I know I shouldn't let him, but it all happens so
gradually, and by the time I put my hand on his to
pull him away he's already holding my bare breast
and it's too late. So I let him. And then he pushes off
the shoulder strap and I keep my eyes tight shut because I don't want to see myself undressed like that.
He lifts his head slightly and I know he's looking and
I feel ashamed, but I think of the naked people on the
beach and then it's not so bad. Now his hand starts to
slide down across my stomach, and I grab it tight.

"No, please, I don't want you to do that," I say,
louder than I expected.

"Don't be afraid," he says, and starts to kiss me
more.

"Please . . ." His hand slips out of my grip, but I
push it away again.

"It's okay," he says.

No, it's not. But I don't say that. I just keep pushing

his hand away every time he puts it anyplace under
my waistline.

He puts it.

I push it.

He puts it.

I push it. This goes on till I think I might start to
laugh, except I'm beginning to get kind of angry. Now
I pull up my shoulder strap and sit straight up. "I
don't want you to do that," I say, and it's really crazy
because here it is, my body, and he's annoyed that he
can't do what he wants to it. Unreal. And he really is
annoyed, like it was his.

"I'm not doing anything. I'm just touching you."
He lies as if I don't know what he's trying to do.

"Then please don't touch me."

"Don't be afraid."

"I'm not afraid. I just don't want you to do that."

"You mean this?" And he puts is hand on my waist.

"Not that."

And he moves his hand farther down my leg and
says, "This?"

And I say, "You know where," and he says, "No,
show me," and I say, "I'm not going to because you
know," and he says, no, really he doesn't, and this stupid conversation goes on and we discuss my body like
it was a map and he can touch here and he can't touch
there and it turns out that he owns the entire northern
half down to someplace around Tennessee and I own
the rest. For now anyway. And it turns into a sort of
cute conversation and I don't know why but I don't
even really feel embarrassed.

Then I say I have to go, and he pushes me back
down and starts to kiss me again and we neck for a
while longer, but he tries all the same stuff I told him
not to again and finally I get up and say I really have
to get back.

He sort of pulls himself together, facing the water,
and shoves his hands into his pockets. Steffi and I

have discussed this a million times about how boys put their hands in their pockets so you can't see they have an erection.

I sort of sneak a peek, but it works—the hands in the pockets, I mean—I don't see a thing.

We start walking up the dock toward the shore, and I'm hoping Jim will want to walk me home, and lucky me, he does. Except all the way home he keeps stopping to pull me to the side of the walkway to kiss me. A couple of times people come by and he doesn't even stop, and I can hear them giggling about us. If only someone from school could see us. Someone like Gloria.

I try to keep away from the lights because I must look a mess. My hair is a horror and my face feels like somebody walked on it. We kiss goodnight in front of the house, and then he says he'll call me tomorrow night. Isn't that the most fabulous thing in the whole world? Jim wants to see me again. I think he must really like me. He writes down my phone number and then he goes.

I watch him until he's out of sight, which only takes half a second because the street is pitch-black. It's got to be at least two in the morning, and I'm probably the only person awake on the whole block. It's dead quiet. Not a light on.

Up till now I haven't let myself think too much about what a disgusting awful underhanded thing I was doing—sneaking out, I mean—because if I really thought about it I know I wouldn't have done it. And I know I absolutely *had* to because it was crucial—I mean, not even just for my whole summer but maybe even for my whole life. I guess that sounds a little much, but still it *was* very important to me. Suddenly all my reasons sound crummy. How come it's all falling apart now just because I'm scared? And I am, too. In fact, I'm freaking out at the thought of trying to get back into my room, especially since it means tiptoeing up two flights of creaky stairs.

I take off my sandals and gently, very gently, turn the handle on the screen door. It opens silently. Good door. Now for the front door. Again I gently squeeze down on the handle, turning it quietly all the way to the left and push. Nothing. Wrong way, dummy. I wipe my sweaty palm on my jeans and grab the handle again and this time turn it all the way to the right and push. Still nothing. I'm not in a panic because no one locks their doors on Fire Island. So it must be just a little stuck. Probably because of the heat and the dampness and all.

It's going to be tough shoving it hard enough without making any noise. I put my shoulder against the door and start pushing with my whole weight. It doesn't move. Now I wedge my feet under the porch railing and with both hands, using the railing for leverage, push the door. Nothing happens. If I didn't have to worry about making noise I could just get back and ram it the way they do in the movies. Even though I'm getting very sweaty and very nervous I calm myself enough to try thinking straight. First thing I've got to find out is exactly where the door is actually stuck, top or bottom.

I check the top first. No problem there. And the bottom seems pretty free, so that means it must be caught in the middle, which is a funny place for a door to be stuck . . . unless what's sticking it isn't just sticking . . . it's locked. Help! I can't believe it. They absolutely never lock their door. Unless . . . oh, no! I did it myself when I turned the door latch sneaking out. I wasn't opening it, I was locking it!

Suddenly I'm so panicked that I have to sit down just to catch my breath. It's horrendous. I can't believe that I'm actually stuck out here and there's no way I can open that door.

Then it hits me.

The windows!

I jump up and run around to the kitchen window, which I know was open all day long. I'm right, it's still open, except that I can't get to the stupid thing because the goddamn screen is on and the only way to get past the screen is to take the whole thing off and there are some dumb things holding it from the inside. It's hopeless. I'm finished. It's all over.

The almost summer of Victoria Martin.

Fired after three brilliant days.

And shamed.

The whole thing is so grotesquely embarrassing. And then, on top of everything else, my parents will have to know. How could I do such a dumb thing? And then be jerky enough to get caught.

I'm crying. Well, naturally, what else am I going to do?

All I figure I've got are two choices and they both stink. First one is I can stay here until the morning. But that's no good because it's going to be a mess when DeeDee comes in to wake me up and I'm not there. Besides, then they'll think I stayed out all night long, which is worse than waking Cynthia up now—and what difference does it really make? Either way I've had it. So I take choice Number Two. I ring the bell.

Do you know what it's like to ring a doorbell at two in the morning when the whole world is sleeping? It sounds like a nine-alarm fire.

I make a quick try at coming up with a plausible story but nothing sounds even half good so I decide to tell the truth, if she's even interested by then.

I can see the lights going on in Cynthia's bedroom, then the hall light, and then she's at the door. This is so awful.

"Victoria!" she says, opening the door. And boy, is

she stunned and confused. "Victoria! What are you doing out here?"

"I don't have a key," I say, postponing the inevitable.

"The door isn't locked."

"Yeah, it is." Wouldn't it be nice if she just forgot everything else and we stood around and talked about the locked door.

"But we never lock the"—she didn't forget—"door. What are you doing out here anyway?"

"Well, it's sort of a long story."

"Why don't you just come in here and start telling me?" And there's a whole big change in her tone. Not good either.

We go into the living room and I pick the worst chair in the room and sit at the edge of it. She sits opposite me. If only there really was something easy like a nine-alarm fire.

"Okay, Victoria, let's have it from the beginning. What are you doing out at two-thirty in the morning?"

"I don't think it's two-thirty yet."

"All right," she says, looking at her watch, "out at two-twenty-five in the morning, when you're supposed to be home in bed? I mean, what *is* going on here?" By now she's really rolling and nothing's going to stop her. "You know you have a one o'clock curfew and what's even worse you just take off in the middle of the night without a word to anyone. I can't believe you'd do such a thing! It's so damned dishonest. Victoria, what's gotten into you?"

"I'm sorry," I say, because I really am.

"Where were you?"

"Out."

"Out where? With whom? What's going on? Don't make me pull it out of you. For goodness' sakes, I think I deserve a proper explanation. After all, I am responsible for you while you're living in my house."

I start to answer but she goes right on. "What if I weren't home? Would you have just sneaked out and left my children alone? How can I believe that you wouldn't? After this, how can I believe anything you say or do?"

"I'm really sorry," I say, "and I would never, ever, go out and leave the kids alone. I made sure you were in bed way before I even thought of going. I was only out an hour and a half."

"Where were you?"

I try to answer her, but the minute I open my mouth I start to cry.

"All right, Victoria, calm down and tell me everything. I'm not a monster. If it's possible to understand, I will. Now please start from the beginning."

"Well . . . it's this boy," I begin, and it's really rough. "I know him from the city and I like him . . . a lot. Actually, I think I love him . . . except naturally he doesn't know it because we only just met. I guess it's all pretty dumb, isn't it?"

"Not really," Cynthia says, and it's crazy, but I think she might understand. "Go on, Victoria, let's hear the whole thing."

"There's another complication," I tell her. "He already has a girl friend, but she's really awful except she's very pretty. I personally don't see it but almost everyone else seems to think she's absolutely beautiful. Anyway, he can't be all that nuts about her because he's definitely interested in me. That's why I *had* to go out tonight. I've been working up to this since before school ended, and finally, today, he asked me out. Sort of."

"What do you mean 'sort of'?"

"Well, it wasn't exactly a formal date. It was more like asking me casually if I was going to be at The Monkey tonight. But I could tell that he was really saying that he wanted me to come, so I *had* to be there. It was my big chance."

"And I said you couldn't go."

"But you didn't know how important it was."

"Then why didn't you tell me?"

"I didn't feel right asking you to change all your plans just for me, and besides, I guess I was kind of embarrassed about asking. Then I fell asleep and when I woke up you were asleep and I felt funny about waking you, and besides, I didn't expect to stay out that long. And there were some other things I didn't expect to do either."

She looks a little alarmed, so I reassure her that I didn't mean that I had sex with him.

"Absolutely not," I say. "I just got sort of carried away. But I didn't think I would because—well, I never did before. But that's the way it's been with Jim. All the things I plan and figure out for myself fall apart the minute he comes into the picture. I can't understand why that happens."

"I don't think I can tell you why, but I can swear it happens and not just to you," she says.

"You too?" I can't picture Cynthia being out of control.

Cynthia stops for a moment and looks hard at me as if she's deciding whether she can trust me.

"Yes," she finally says, "with Jed. All the time, but it's over now."

"I'm sorry," I say.

She shrugs and throws out her hands like, "What are you going to do?" "I guess it was the hardest time of my life," she says. "I let it happen. I let myself be the victim, sitting around in misery and tears waiting for the next blow. And they came. One woman after another. Finally one day I started to get angry, and then I got furious, and I realized, my God, I'm finally alive. I threw him out, and even though it was like tearing something out of my body I survived it. And I'm okay now. I'm still angry but I'm not bitter. Bitter is just more self-pity and that's not for me anymore."

See how you don't know about people? I always thought of Cynthia as sort of nice but mostly lazy and self-centered, and I guess she is that, too, but she's definitely a lot more. She's sensitive and understanding and a whole different person to me now, and I like her much more and I even respect her. I feel like we're friends, really and truly friends.

"Even though your situation with Jim is different," she tells me, "in one way it's the same. You're letting yourself be taken advantage of. You're being the victim. Don't let it happen."

I say I'm not going to, but I'm not really sure because I don't feel angry or anything like what she feels about Jed. All I feel is in love with Jim. And I want very much to stay out here, and if only she'll forgive me I wouldn't care how much work I had to do or anything.

"All I can do is advise you about your love life," she says, "but when it comes to your job, that's a different story. There I can lay down the law. You did a lousy thing tonight, and the only way I would even consider allowing you to stay on is if I have your solemn word that this kind of thing will never happen again."

"Oh, it won't! I swear!" More tears. I can't help it, I'm a very emotional person. Besides, these are sort of happy tears. I think I'm out from under.

"Well, I hope I'm not making a mistake. . . ."

"You're not. I promise!"

"Okay then. We'll forget the whole thing."

"Thank you, Cynthia. I really appreciate . . ."

"I don't know how much you're going to appreciate it when DeeDee starts pulling at you at seven in the morning. You know it's after three. We better get to bed."

"Thanks, Cynthia . . . a lot." And she turns out the light and we both go up to bed.

She's really a terrific person. I don't know how fast

I'd be to forgive someone who did such a sneaky thing to me. She's sensational and so understanding.

On the other hand, I hear it's pretty hard to replace a mother's helper after the season starts. And DeeDee does get up kind of early.

I shoot upstairs. Reprieved!

Boy, this room will be so terrific in August! I know I keep saying that, but I know everyone will be so jealous when we start to get those cold nights. Right now, of course, it's stifling.

I throw off my clothes and plop down on the bed. What a night! I wish Steffi were here so I could talk to her about it. Except maybe I wouldn't talk about everything. Now that it's over, I'm beginning to feel a little funny, sort of embarrassed and—I don't know— maybe I shouldn't have let him go so far on the first date. Except Cynthia didn't seem all that surprised. Oh, God, it really was the first date and I let him put his hand under my clothes. Oh, I'm beginning to feel awful. Why did I do that? It was all right to do some necking, but that was really heavy petting, and now he probably thinks he can make out with me anytime he wants. I wish I didn't let him put his hand under my clothes. I don't know why I let him. I never let anyone before. Oh, it's so embarrassing. How am I going to ever face him again? He must think I'm really easy. Steffi would, too, if I told her. But I'm not going to. I'm not going to tell anyone else. But what if *he* does? Suppose he tells Barry?

Maybe he went back to the The Monkey and maybe he's telling his friends now and they're all laughing and talking about me the way they do Sheila McCauley. She's the class "easy." I'd die if they talked about me like that. I'd never go back to school or anything, ever again.

Jim wouldn't do that. He's not that kind of guy. I know it, I think. I hope. Boy, that would really be low.

Even though I don't think he would be that low, still it takes me forever to fall asleep because I can't keep my mind from thinking what if he was a big-mouth, and then I keep tracing it down to how it even got back to my family. I'm an expert at self-torture. The last thing I remember is dawn.

13

It doesn't make any difference to DeeDee that it's Sunday, she's in there pulling on me before seven, same as usual. No fighting it, so I struggle up. I must be getting used to the room because this is the first morning I don't bump my head on the ceiling when I sit up. I bump my knee.

Among the piles of dirty dishes there's a note from Cynthia saying we should not wake her up because she's exhausted from all the nighttime activity, but she'd just love it if I could just straighten the living room a tiny bit. She always leaves the cutest notes, like this one starts off, "Help! Help!"

I give DeeDee her usual breakfast, which she wastes half of as usual. No matter how little I give her she leaves more than half. While she's eating, I start to clean up the living room. It looks like the party Cynthia had the night before was great from the horrendous mess they left. In the middle of cleaning up, David comes down and I give him his peanut butter sandwich and go back to work. The kids watch TV for the next couple of hours until I finish everything. I want to do it right because I'm really sensitive after last night.

After breakfast I start to get the kids into their bathing suits when the phone rings. Don't let it be Mr. Landry, please.

It isn't. It's my mom. We have a sort of strange conversation. At least from my end it's a little weird. Naturally she wants to know all about my job, and if she called yesterday I would have given her an earful. I had planned to do some fancy moaning about all the work Cynthia dumps on me, but after last night's horrendous fiasco I play it very cool.

"Cynthia's terrific, really, Mom," I say. "I'm crazy about her kids too. It's the best summer job I ever had." That's a little overboard, seeing this is my first summer job. "I love it out here. Everything is absolutely perfect, really super. Boy, it's just great, I tell you this is fantastic, sensational. . . ."

"Victoria?"

"Yeah, Mom?"

"What's wrong?"

"I must be getting my period," I say, thinking faster than I ever thought in my whole life.

"Are you sure that's all it is?"

"Well . . ."

"Well, what?"

"Well, I didn't think it was going to be so hard," and even though I said I wasn't going to let it happen, everything starts running out of my mouth—all the things that Cynthia makes me do (if you can't complain to your mother who can you complain to?). I go on and on about the laundry and the dishes and the cleaning and everything, and I can tell my mother is absolutely on my side. In fact, she's so much on my side that she's beginning to hate Cynthia and in two seconds she's going to tell me to quit and come home. Well, I certainly don't want that, so I do a fast double about-face and go right into how, of course, Cynthia is right there working along beside me, she and the kids, and by the time I finish I make it sound as though all I do is sit around polishing my nails while everyone waits on me.

"It sounds terrible," my mother says, not one bit fooled. "But if you're so anxious to stay, try it for an-

other week. And don't be shy, Victoria. If you think
she's being unfair, tell her."

My mother makes it sound so easy, but it isn't like
that when you're a kid *and* an employee. I tell her I'll
talk to Cynthia, but I know I'll never have the guts.

Then my mom tries to feel better because except for
mistakes like last night I really am doing a pretty terrific job, and even though it's hard, it makes me feel
kind of proud. If only I could handle the other part of
my life the way I clean the house, I'd be in business.

"I love you, Mommy," I tell her.

"Love you too, sugar. Now what's up for this afternoon? Are you going to the beach or does she have you
scrubbing the walls?"

I laugh and tell her that we were just getting into
our suits.

"Have you been swimming yet?"

"Are you kidding? David is a water demon. We go
in four, five times a day."

"And you have to come back to the house every
time to change your suit?"

"Well . . ."

"Oh." There's a tiny silence while my mother wres-
tles with the idea of her fifteen-year-old daughter risking her life sitting around in a wet bathing suit. Finally she sort of mumbles something like, "I guess
that's the way it has to be," and I know it's beginning
to happen. I'm really growing up.

"Don't forget to take those vitamin pills Daddy gave
you, and watch out for the sun, and . . ."

And she's off and rolling again. The rest of the conversation is filled with warnings to watch out for this
and that and news of everyone back home (what big
things could have happened in four days?) . Plus not
to forget that it's really very important to Daddy
about me staying alone overnight. Did I talk to Cynthia about that yet? I lie and say it's all settled. I
promise myself to bring it up in the next couple of

days for sure. Then she says how I should make sure to write a nice long letter to Nina.

Sure thing. "Dear toad . . ."

After I hang up from talking with my mother, I take the kids down to the beach. Funny, I really wasn't homesick until that telephone call, but just talking to my mother suddenly makes me feel very alone. Maybe it's because even though mostly it bugs me to pieces, still it's kind of nice having someone worrying and caring so much about you. Isn't it ridiculous? I miss my mommy. Oh, God, I sound just like DeeDee. The thought tickles me enough to make me feel better.

By the time I get down to the beach Dana and Anita are already there, and of course they're dying to know what happened to me at The Monkey last night. Naturally I don't tell them anything much. I pretend that Jim and I danced and then went out to the end of the pier to talk. They both think Jim is something else and want to know all about him and when am I going to see him again. That's a little tough to answer, but I tell them probably tomorrow. That's Monday, my day off.

"Where's he taking you?" Dana wants to know.

"Well, we're not sure yet," I tell them, "but we might have a picnic dinner and then hit The Monkey later." That's not really a lie because if we do go out together tomorrow he'd probably love to do that.

We rap for an hour or so while the kids play around, and then it's time to go home for lunch.

There's a beautiful four-hundred-page thank-you note waiting for me on the kitchen table. Four hundred pages of explicit instructions. First, though, she says I did an A-1 job and she's going to love me forever for saving her from waking up to such a huge mess and that she's off to the Hendersons' for a brunch party and not to wait for her for lunch. Then she says a couple of other things about what to feed the kids and would I please get a few things started for dinner. She tells me exactly how to clean the chicken and prepare it for the oven and how to do the vegetables and clean the shrimp and make the salad (she must be having company) and everything. She must have taken twenty minutes just to write the note.

DeeDee goes in for a nap and David eats his lunch watching TV. It looks like rain. Just as well because dinner is going to take me a while to get ready and at least the kids won't be hassling me to go to the beach.

The phone rings. I leap for it because it has to be Jim. It isn't. But lucky for me, at least it isn't Mr. Landry again. It's Barry.

"I looked for you last night at The Monkey," I say. I want to find out if he was there and if he saw Jim.

"We had company last night," he says. "My cousins from Connecticut came, so I had to hang around. Were you there?"

Obviously he didn't speak to Jim yet so he doesn't know, or maybe he did speak to Jim and Jim didn't say anything because of the way Barry feels about me. "For a while," I tell him.

"How'd you like it?"

"It's okay." I'm not feeling as cool as I sound.

"Hey, listen, if you're off tomorrow, do you want to come over for some tennis?"

"In the afternoon?" Jim works till five so I might as well.

"Around two," Barry says.

"Sure, that'd be great."

"Yeah?" Like he's really surprised. I guess he still likes me. Poor Dana.

"Sure," I say, and he tells me where his house is and how to get there.

I tell him I have to run to close the windows because now the rain is really coming down. Too late. The whole side of my bed is soaking wet. I don't know how so much rain came in that tiny window. I change the sheets and hang the blanket up to dry and come back downstairs to finish cleaning the shrimp. Gross. There must be fifty of them. It'll take me forever.

The phone rings again and I almost tell David to pick it up because my hands are gloppy from the shrimp, but then I remember Mr. Landry and dry them off and answer it myself.

"Hello?" I say.

"You the mother's helper?" It's a man's voice. I know exactly who it is and my stomach sinks.

"Yes, it's me, Victoria."

"Right. Listen, Victoria, how are my grandchildren?"

"Fine. just fine."

David strolls in to see who I'm talking to. "Who's that?" he wants to know.

"Nobody," I tell him. "It's for me."

"That David you're talking to?" Mr. Landry asks, and I'm not about to lie so I say yes, it's David.

"Please let me talk to him." And I can't really say no. After all, I let him talk to DeeDee, and besides, I already decided that I'm not going to do what someone says if I think they're absolutely wrong. Of course, now I have to think of a good story for David so that he doesn't tell his mother. She'd really be furious if she ever found out. But I have to take that risk because kids have to be able to talk to their grandfather, especially if they love him the way David and DeeDee love theirs. I don't usually make big important decisions like this, I mean with adults involved, so it's kind of scary.

"David," I say, "I was wrong. It's for you."

"For me?" He jumps up and runs over to the phone. "Hello? Grandpa!" Then to me, all excited, "It's my Grandpa!" See, they really do love him a whole lot. ". . . Yeah, I'm okay. When are you coming out? . . . How come not for so long? . . . But you said you were going to take us fishing . . . But you said . . . I don't want to go fishing with Victoria, I want to go fishing with you. . . ." And he looks like he's going to cry. "Please, Grandpa, I miss you. . . ."

Oh, I feel awful.

"Can I come see you? . . . How come? . . . Mommy could take me. She's going into the city Tuesday and then she could take me to your house. . . . I don't know, she has an appointment, I guess . . . She said she has to make an early train. . . ." Then he turns to me. "What time is Mommy coming home Tuesday night?"

"I don't know," I tell him. "Late, I think. Why?"

"Victoria says late, Grandpa . . . You will? . . . Oh, boy, terrific." And he starts jumping up and down. "Victoria! My Grandpa's gonna see me on Tuesday!"

Oh, no! "Give me the phone for a minute, David," I say. "I want to say something." And I practically grab the phone out of his hand.

"Mr. Landry? Don't hang up, I have to talk to you." And then I turn to David and say to him, "I forgot to tell you but Steven from across the street was here before and he wants you to come over."

"Tell my grandpa to come out early," he says.

"I will. You better get over to Steven's because he wanted to show you something."

"What is it?" he asks.

"He didn't say what it was but he said he would let you hold it." God, I hate to lie. Still, it was good enough to make him shoot right out the door.

"Mr. Landry, Cynthia's going to be very angry that I even let you talk to the kids, but when she finds out that you're coming out she won't go to the city at all and then she's going to be furious with me."

"We won't tell her."

"I can't do that. That would be really dishonest and I don't think that's fair."

"All right," he says, "I won't come." I'm surprised that

I convinced him so easily, but he must be a really nice person if the kids love him so much, and they do.

"Thanks a lot, Mr. Landry. I'm really sorry that it has to be like this. If you hold on one sec I'll get David and you can tell him yourself," and I race across the street toward Steven's house and practically run smack into David on his way home.

"Nobody's home," he tells me.

"Come on, quick, you're grandpa's still on the phone and he wants to say something to you."

And we both run into the house and David picks up the phone and says, "Hello," and then he holds the receiver out to me and says, "There's no one there."

And I take it and, sure enough, there's a dial tone. We must have been disconnected, or else that nice old man purposely hung up so he would stick me with having to explain why he can't come Tuesday.

"We must have gotten cut off," I say. "But he wanted me to give you the message that he's afraid he can't make it for Tuesday."

"How come?" David's really disappointed.

"He has to go to the doctor."

Now he's worried. "Is Grandpa sick or something?"

"Oh, no, he's absolutely fine, but he has to take his friend who's very, very sick."

"Mr. Whiteman?"

"Uh-uh," I say with a shake of my head. "This is a friend you don't know. But your grandfather said he knew that you would understand and not to say anything about his call to your mother because he wants to surprise her when he comes out."

Boy, he's really crushed, and he keeps asking me things like maybe his grandpa can come out after he takes his friend to the doctor, and then a million questions about how come he can't come out on Wednesday and then Thursday, and the kid is really and truly disappointed. I feel like a rat, and on top of all that, Steven wasn't home and now he wants to know what Steven had for him to hold.

"I think it was his new book on Vitamins and Children's Growth."

"That stinks. I don't even want to see that dumb book. He's a jerk."

"I told him you wouldn't care." But he doesn't even listen because he's back into the TV.

I go back to the shrimp which look like they had a few baby shrimp while I was gone. It takes me another hour and a half to finish cleaning and deveining the shrimp, and I'm halfway into chopping the onions and crying my eyes out when Cynthia comes in. DeeDee hears her and comes downstairs. I go into the living room, and while Cynthia's talking to DeeDee I give David a little poke and remind him not to say anything about his grandfather's call because of the surprise.

Cynthia comes into the kitchen and makes a big fuss about how great I cleaned the shrimp and how I'm the best shrimp cleaner in the country, and I told you, she really is appreciative about things. So would I be if somebody cleaned a truckload of shrimp for me. As soon as I finish the onions, she says, leave the rest to her (except that it's all done) and would I please take the wagon down to the grocery store and pick up some beer and soda.

"David! DeeDee! Go help Victoria with the soda," she calls to them just as I'm about to slip out of the house. I don't know why she thinks they're such a help. I wish I could tell her it's easier to get it without them.

No luck. Naturally they jump in the wagon like always. It's not so bad going there but coming back with the kids and the soda it's horrendous. I have to figure out a way to get them to walk sometimes.

The phone rings just when we get back, and I dump my packages down and grab it. It's got to be Jim.

"Hello? . . . Is Victoria there?" It's him.

"Hi," I say, "it's me."

"Yeah, well, I'm working now so I have to make this fast. Something's come up so I won't be able to see you for a few days, but I'll call you sometime around the end of the week. Okay?"

"Sure." I'm disappointed but he *did* call even if it was to say he couldn't see me. That's a whole lot better than not calling at all. I told you he's a very considerate person.

"Well, see you around," he says.

"Okay, see you." And we both hang up.

It's not so bad anyway because I probably wouldn't be able to get out tonight so it's just as well. He called. That's really what counts.

The company turns out to be two other women and one guy and the food is delicious. The kids and I eat first in the kitchen and then after I put them to bed I come down and do the dishes for us and for the company. It's only seven people but it feels like a million dishes because they don't have a dishwasher.

Cynthia offers to help, but she's a little high from the drinks so I just tell her, don't worry, I can handle it myself. She looks a little surprised, then she says, "You're a doll," and goes back to some crazy game they are playing, a kind of porno-charades that they think is the funniest thing since the belly button.

I think maybe after the dishes Cynthia is going to suggest that I can go out for a walk, but she says she's probably going out so I get into bed with a book and before I know it my eyes are starting to close. Tomorrow's my day off and I'm going to sleep till twelve. At least. Horray!

14

"No, DeeDee, it's my day off." I tell her when she starts climbing in my bed, but a lot of good that does. She says she's not hungry, she just wants to sleep with me. I can't throw her off the bed so I move over and she squeezes in, and that's not easy because it's a very narrow bed and I'm always hanging off. I try to get back to sleep but she keeps jumping around and telling me how she'll be very quiet and how she's going to sleep and all that, so finally I get up.

"Now let's eat," she says, and as long as I'm up I might as well give her breakfast.

David comes down the usual time, and I remind him not to say anything to DeeDee about the phone call because she's too young to keep a secret. He likes that. I thought he would. Actually she's terrific about her own secret grandpa thing. And I know she didn't forget because all she wants to do all day is go get the mail.

Cynthia's still sleeping and the kids want to go to the beach and so I figure I might as well take them. I guess you can call it the high cost of sneaking out.

The usual group is at the beach and they're surprised to see me.

"Hey," Dana says, "I thought you have Mondays off."

"I do," I tell her. "But I wasn't doing anything this morning so I figured I might as well bring the kids to the beach."

Dana and Anita say I really shouldn't do that because I could screw it up for everybody, but I tell them that Cynthia is really very nice to me and so it's no big deal to me and besides, it's not as though she asked me.

Anita wantes to know what Cynthia does that's so great, and I tell them I can't think of anything specific right this minute but she's a very appreciative person, and I'm about to tell them about the notes, how cute they are, but then I think maybe they won't see them that way so I just say, "I don't know . . . things."

We rap about this and that, but I don't mention going to Barry's house today because I know Dana sort of digs him. Funny, I'm not even very excited about going. It's practically that I feel I have to. Still, it did kind of bug me a little that day he was paying so much attention to Dana. You know, the day he and Jim were surfing. Maybe I just don't like to lose any of my admirers.

I get back with the kids at about eleven-thirty and Cynthia had to go pick up her shoes (her note says) and she'll be back in a second.

She must have gotten held up, so while I'm waiting, I give the kids lunch and do her morning dishes. She doesn't get back until almost two because that dumb guy at the shoe store didn't finish fixing her shoes and she had to wait all this time while he did them because he closes in the afternoon and she needed them for work tomorrow. I can see she was really aggravated to hold me up like that but I tell her it's all right. I was only going to play tennis and he'll wait.

I love the tennis clothes almost more than actually playing. I have this terry-cloth skirt that's really cute. I just wish my knees weren't so bony and stick-outy. I should wash my hair, but I don't feel like it, and besides, it's only Barry.

His house is beautiful. He must be really rich because it's like one of those houses you see in magazines and it's right on the water with a beach in the back and a tennis court in the front. Barry is rallying with some kid, a girl about Nina's age. He stops as soon as he sees me and comes over to the gate door.

"Hi," he says.

"Hi." I smile. "Hey, don't let me stop your game. Go on, I'll sit here and watch for a while." And I throw my stuff down on a wooden bench.

"That's okay, we were just killing time. You want to hit some balls?" He completely ignores the girl.

"What about her?"

"That's nobody," he says, almost surprised that I mentioned her. "That's just my sister." And then he shouts to her that we're going to use the court—just like that. She shrugs and starts to walk over toward us.

"Can I have winners?" she asks.

"Hey, Kathy," Barry says impatiently, "don't bug me. I told you I was going to use the court all afternoon."

"Can I watch?"

"Oh, for God's sake! Do you have to?"

"I won't say anything. I'm just gonna sit here and watch."

"Let her watch," I say, "I don't mind." Amazing how easy it is when it's not *your* sister.

"Yeah, wait till you see what a pain in the neck she is." He says it like she's not even there.

"Is it okay if I move your stuff?" Kathy asks me. She's tough like Nina. You can insult Nina and say anything you want right in front of her, and nothing, she never even gets embarrassed.

"Beat it, Kathy," he tells her.

"It's a free country. I can stand where I want." And she puts her hands on her hips and just stands there. I think this kid must be taking lessons from Nina. Now he's the one who's getting embarrassed.

"Hey, Barry, it's okay with me, really." I jump in, trying to save the situation. "Let her watch."

"See, even she doesn't care, big shot," Kathy says, and she really is a pain. I think I'll have no trouble creaming Barry, he's so thrown from this whole scene.

I'm wrong. He may be thrown, but he blitzes me anyway. He's a fabulous player. We rally a few times and you can see he's trying to hit balls that I can return, which is very nice of him, and he's so good that they come in straight and I'm hitting them with no trouble at all, or hardly any. We don't even see when Kathy gets bored and leaves.

After a while we both start clowning around, imitating ballet dancers and ninety-year-old people playing tennis. Then Barry does a zoo thing where he's a monkey and a chicken, and I know it sounds like the dumbest thing but it's absolutely hysterical. I laugh so hard I keep collapsing on the ground. Finally I have to run off the court because if I don't I swear I'm going to wet my pants—I mean, he is so wild. I think he could be a comedian.

"How about a swim?" he says, coming over to where I've thrown myself down on the grass trying to catch my breath.

"Yes, help," I gasp and we both head for the pool.

It's terrific being with Barry when he doesn't push all that heavy stuff on me. In fact, I laugh more with him than with Steffi even, and she and I spend half the time being hysterical about something or someone. It's as though Barry is an old friend—I mean that's how comfortable I feel with him. I love to have boys for friends but it's always hard because mostly they don't want to be just friends. Too bad.

The inside of his house is even better than the outside. It's all bright green and white, and it looks clean and crisp. I love it. I change into my bikini and head for the pool. It's in the back of the house on a wooden deck facing the ocean. The water is bright aqua and so delicious-looking I dive right in.

You know how in all the ads girls look so fabulous

after they come out of the water even with dripping hair? Not me. I look like real people do when they're wet, only worse.

Kathy comes out with a friend and we all play some dumb kid games in the pool and have a great time, chasing each other and diving in and all that. At one point I'm "it," and I'm tearing around the pool chasing Patty, Kathy's friend, and she's screaming, and I'm just about to grab her when out of the corner of my eye I see a figure. A girl's figure. A great girl's figure and long blond hair, and I stop in midair.

"I win! I win!" Patty shouts, and I know without looking that I lose and it isn't just the game.

"Hi, everybody," says Gloria, and my heart actually stops for a second and then starts pounding so hard I can barely hear myself think.

I turn around and look and there she is, looking perfect. Her blond hair catching the sun makes her look like one of those religious pictures where there's like a halo of light around the angel's head. Even if I'm going a little too far, still she looks fabulous. Her bikini is a light blue velour that probably matches her vacant eyes.

And right behind her is Jim. What a blow. So that's the special something that came up. It's not that I thought we were going steady or anything like that, but . . . I don't know, I guess I just didn't expect to see Gloria out here. I can hardly bring my eyes up to his face, I feel so embarrassed. He should be just as embarrassed as me except when I do look at him he isn't at all, but he does look surprised to see me.

By now my face is so burning red that all I can do to save myself is jump into the pool. I dive and I'm so freaked out that I do a horrendous bellywop. Why do I always look bad when it's so important to look good? Anyway, I keep swimming around, stalling for time. I hear Barry calling my name, but I pretend I don't. What if I just stayed here . . . forever? After a while

I'd be a curiosity and people would come over to Barry's just to see the girl in the pool. I'd get my name in the *Guinness Book of World Records*.

"Victoria!" It's Barry calling me. I'm floating with my eyes closed, but he knows I can hear him, so I turn around and swim toward his side.

"I'm going to put up a barbecue," Barry says. "Can you stay?"

This whole thing is bad news and I know I should get out fast but I can't. I want to be with Jim, even if Gloria is here too.

"Sure," I tell Barry, "I'd love to." And I pull myself out of the water. "It's great," I say to Gloria in my friendly, outgoing voice.

"It looks terrific but it kills my hair." She doesn't even sound bitchy like the last time I met her. "I have the same problem as you do," she goes on. "My hair looks horrible when it's wet." I was wrong.

"Anybody want a Coke?" Barry asks.

"Yeah, I'll take one," Jim says, and Barry goes in the house to get them. "How do you like it out here?" For a second I don't even realize Jim is talking to me. It's like he hasn't seen me since the first day at the pier. Like there was no night on the pier. I guess it's because of Gloria.

"I love it out here." I play along.

"How's Cynthia?" Gloria asks, and her voice actually is rather pleasant. I wonder why I hate it so much.

"She's terrific," I tell her. "Really super and I love the job."

"I'll just bet," she says, really snotty.

"Where are you staying out here?" I ask, and she practically laughs in my face.

"You have to be kidding. Where do you think I'm staying?" And she looks at Jim and nods toward me and shakes her head like I'm some kind of a moron. Jim doesn't say anything but he looks very uncomfortable. How am I supposed to know who she's staying with? But she obviously wants me to guess, so like a dope I say, "Relatives?" And she breaks up.

"I don't know. . . ." She's all full of giggles, burying her head in Jim's chest. "Are you my relative?"

I don't believe it. She's just putting me on.

"Hi, cuz," she says cutesy-poo-like, poking Jim in the stomach with her little finger.

"Yeah. . . ." Jim says, blushing a little but still kind of enjoying it.

Unreal! She's not putting me on. She really *is* staying with him! All I can think of is that she's only a year older than me and she's practically living with someone. So what if it's only for a couple of days, that's still pretty wild for only a high school junior. That's all she is, you know, a junior. I'm in shock but I disguise it with a real cool face and a kind of "that's nice, so what else is new" look. I'm not about to give her the satisfaction of knowing that she's blowing my mind.

"Sor-ry, didn't mean to freak you out," she says right into my hopeless see-through face. What I'd really like to do is let her know what her lover boy has been doing before she got here. But I can't because it's not so great for me either. I don't say anything but I give Jim a look like he's a real two-timer. And he reads me so perfectly he takes off. Right into the pool.

I figure since my hair looks horrible already, as Gloria so kindly reminded me, I have nothing more to lose, so I jump in after him. Anything is better than standing there listening to that.

I know that it's rotten for him to do that to Gloria, but I'm the only one who feels lousy. After all, it's not so bad for her—she doesn't even know. How could he do that, pretend to be so interested in me when all along he knew he had this relationship with someone else?

I'm swimming around thinking all these angry

thoughts and I don't even notice where I'm going so, sure enough, I swim right into his feet. It's always like that with me. I mean, it might be sort of romantic if I accidentally swam into his arms, but his feet? I'm hopeless. Anyway, we both come up to the water, and he sort of grabs me around the waist and says, "You okay?"

I picked up a mouthful of water that I don't feel like spitting out right in front of him so I just nod my head, okay.

He smiles at me. A private, warm, hi-there-honey smile that makes my whole body whoozy. Boy, he just knocks me out. I wish he didn't because I'm beginning to think maybe he's not so great. "Sorry for that," he says, nodding back toward Gloria.

Maybe he was trapped into having her out. I mean, maybe he promised a long time ago, before me anyway, and now he couldn't get out of it. It could happen that way, you know. I decide that that's exactly what did happen, and I smile.

Mistake. I still had a mouthful of water. Beautiful the way it comes running out from between my teeth and down my chin. But Jim's not turned off.

"Too much," he says and starts to laugh. Nice like. *Very* nice. I sneak a look over my shoulder to see if Gloria is watching and she is. But so what? There's no law against talking, is there? Still, I cool it a little and start swimming around.

After a while we come out of the water and Gloria must sense something because she's really icy to me. Maybe she just plain doesn't like me. That's okay with me. I don't like her.

I head for the bathroom to make repairs on this gross hair and Gloria follows me. I don't actually turn around to see her, but you know how sometimes you can practically feel somebody behind you? Especially if it's someone you don't want to be there?

Barry's sister, Kathy, gives me directions to the bathroom and hands me a blow-dryer. Hint, hint.

"Want me to help you with your hair?" Gloria asks me, and I try not to look stunned.

"Yeah, sure, if you don't mind."

"No problem," she says. And she plugs it in and starts doing my hair. I'm probably going to end up looking like *I* was plugged in but I'm lousy at saying no.

"What do you think of Jimmy?" she asks.

"Okay, I guess," I say.

"That's all? Boy, he'd be crushed to think there was somebody who didn't think he was gorgeous."

"Well, he *is* very good-looking."

"Nobody knows that better than he does."

"If you think he's so stuck on himself how come you're always hanging out with him?"

"Well . . ." she says. And for the first time her eyes don't look so vacant and she doesn't seem quite so sure of herself.

". . . I guess, maybe, I'm sort of stuck on him too."

She waits for me to make a comment but I can't think of anything nice to say, so she goes on.

"A lot of girls are always throwing themselves at Jimmy." Now she snaps off the blower and looks straight at me. "And he's always nice to them but they don't really have a chance. We've been going together for almost a year now and it's a pretty solid relationship."

I don't say anything because I don't want to hurt her even if I'm not exactly crazy about her.

"It's tough to keep a good thing going when all sorts of girls are always getting in the way," she continues. "But he's only human, you know, so naturally he's going to respond . . . sort of. I don't really feel that threatened. Still, I could do without the interference. I suppose if he wasn't so gorgeous it wouldn't happen—

but then if he wasn't so gorgeous maybe I wouldn't like him so much."

All I can think of is that no matter how blue those eyes are or how silky that hair is I'm glad I'm not Gloria.

But I know what she means. Turns out that fancy hotstuff Gloria is hooked even worse than me. Worse because she knows something funky's going on but she's so knocked out about him that she just sticks around and takes it. I don't think I could ever do that. Don't get me wrong, I don't think what Jim's doing is so great either—I mean, seeing another girl while he's supposed to be going steady. Still, it's probably hard for him to break away from Gloria because it's been so long now.

"One time," Gloria says, and she sounds sort of sad, "way in the beginning when we first started dating, we went to an opening of this off-Broadway play and some guy thought we were movie stars, which freaked us both out. When we told him we weren't, he said we should be and that we made a perfect couple—I mean, we looked so right together, what with the same color hair and all that. Maybe that's not so good. Maybe I'd be better off with someone a little more ordinary. Probably be a lot easier."

It's like she was talking to herself, so I just sit there quietly looking in the mirror.

"What do you think?" she asks me.

"I don't know, I guess you can't always help who you fall for."

"Save the Ann Landers bit," she says. "I meant your hair." Just when I was beginning to like her a little she goes back to the old Gloria bitch. "Well, do you like it or not?"

"Oh . . . it's very nice." I wish I was gutsier. It looks awful and I'm sure she did it on purpose.

"That's okay," I say. "I'll finish up."

"Sure 'nuff," she says, and dumps the blower in my lap, still roaring and plenty hot, and disappears.

I finish up the best I can and go back outside.

Barry is fooling around, trying to light a fire, and everybody is telling him how to do it and naturally no one knows what they're saying. I just sort of melt in with the crowd. Jim gets us all beers and I sip on mine. I don't like beer—in fact, I really hate any kind of alcohol. It tastes awful. A couple of times at holiday dinners at home I've gotten a little giddy on wine but that's all. I guess I'll never be much on drinking unless they come up with something that tastes a whole lot better than Scotch. Ugh!

"I'm going to ride some waves," Jim announces after a while. "Anybody coming?" Gloria takes it as a personal invitation and whines, "Ohhh . . . Jimmy, it's too cold. Brrrr . . ."

She's too much. It must be 90.

"I'll pass on it," Barry tells Jim. "I want to get this fire under control."

Now Jim looks at me. And Gloria looks at me. And Barry looks at me. My mind is racing around in a quick think. I know exactly what I should do. A lot of help that is.

"Sounds good to me," I say, doing the exact opposite, and he says terrific, and before anyone can add another word we both turn and race off toward the beach. I don't care so much about Gloria but I feel a little bad for Barry. I know I didn't come here as his girl friend, but still I wouldn't want him to think I'm trying to get a thing going with Jim right in front of him. After all, all I'm doing is going for a little swim. Oh, who am I kidding!

The water is sensational. It's rough and the undertow is strong but the waves are just perfect for riding. I think Jim is a little surprised at how good I am in the water, especially after someone like Gloria. Bearing that in mind, I show off a little and scare myself half to death a couple of times. I'm actually risking my life to impress Jim. I must be nuts or really crazy in love with him.

We have a super time and he shows me how to ride the waves with our arms around each other, and then he rides the waves with me sitting on his back like I'm on the surfboard. It feels like we're only out there twenty minutes or so, but from the looks of where the sun is it must be a lot longer. We're exhausted when we get out of the water and both of us collapse on the hot sand.

"You swim like a fish," he tells me. What he doesn't know is that I'm not all that good but I never worked so hard at anything in my entire life. It shows what you can do if you really knock yourself out trying. Funny, but in this relationship I seem to be surprising myself all the time.

"Maybe we should go back," I say presently. I start to get up but he pulls me down. "I think the food's probably ready by now," I add.

He starts to kiss me but I pull away and look around, especially back toward the house. Thank goodness nobody's in sight.

"I really thing we should get back," I tell him. "Besides, somebody could be looking. Gloria or somebody."

"Sure," he says, "no big deal. Let's go back."

Then I think maybe he gave up a little too easily. I must be really freaking out. I don't know what I want anymore.

When we get back to the pool nobody's around, so we head toward the house. I get a sinking feeling that it's really late. I mean, we must have been fooling around out there for probably a couple of hours. It feels sevenish.

From the pool you have to go through an enclosed patio. Bad news. The clock says almost seven-thirty. I can't believe we were out that long.

"Hey, Barry! Gloria?" Jim calls their names as we walk into the den. "Where is everybody?" Barry's sister is sprawled on the couch with her friend, watching TV.

"Oh, boy are you two in trouble," she says, the typical brat sister. I shouldn't have wasted my time being nice to her. I can tell she's even worse than Nina.

"Barry around?" Jim asks as though she hadn't said anything.

"Uh-uh." She's an expert. She's going to make him crawl for it.

"Where is he?" Jim finally asks.

"Out," she says, and doesn't even look away from the television.

"What about Gloria?" You can see he's really getting teed off.

Kathy shrugs.

"Now look," Jim says, snapping off the TV, "talk! Where'd everybody go?"

"Barry's out at the ice cream shop. He said he was going to work a couple of hours and Gloria said that she's going home and to tell you . . ." And she stops and smiles up at him.

"Tell me what?" he says, falling right into her trap. Even I can see it's going to be fatal.

"Turn the TV back on first," she says, still with that disgusting grin.

He turns it back on.

"She said to tell you . . ."

"Yeah . . ." he says.

"Drop dead!" And both she and her friend break up and practically fall on the floor in hysterics. Best day they've had since the cat was run over.

Jim charges out the door and I follow him. "Monsters," I tell him. "I know because my sister's just like that."

"I can't stand that kid," he says, and I can see he's aggravated and it's probably not about Kathy. Probably about Gloria. This whole thing is really a mess now. It's not exactly fair because mostly we were just swimming. Oh, who am I fooling? It was awful.

Then he surprises me and instead of going after Gloria he asks me if I want to go over to The Monkey for a while.

I don't know, it's so bad already I don't suppose it's going to be any worse if we go over and have a few dances. So I say yes.

The Monkey is one of those places that is always jammed.

It's not even eight o'clock and you can hardly squeeze in the door. I spot Anita and Dana and they see me and we wave. I'm glad they see I'm with Jim because I told them I would be anyway. At least one thing worked out.

Jim leads me to the dance floor and we start to hustle. They have "Don't Leave Me This Way" on and it's one of my favorites. I know this whole thing's not exactly working the way I planned it, but still, I'm not complaining. I am actually out on a date with Him. I've been waiting for this night since I first saw him last September. He's different than I thought he was but I still think he's outrageous and I really am crazy about him.

The next record is real slow, "You Make Me Feel Brand-New."

He holds me close and we barely move. My head is against his chest and he smells sort of salty and nice. I hope Anita and Dana see us. After all, he is horrendously handsome. Oh, God, everybody's going to just die when we get back to school this fall. Imagine me being Jim Freeman's girl friend. I'll go to all the tennis matches and sit in those special seats right behind the team. That's where their girl friends sit and everybody knows it and looks at you. And then we'll eat together in the lunchroom. Anybody on the varsity team always gets to sit in this side section of the lunchroom that's just reserved for them. It's not really reserved but that's just the way it works out. It will be so fantastic, and then maybe I can even get Steffi a date with one of his friends, and then if they like each other we can double-date. Oh, this year is going to be the greatest in all my life. I just know it.

I'm so into these gorgeous thoughts that I'm not even aware that Jim is holding me tight and whispering something into my hair. Then I lift my head and I bump his chin a tiny bit, which catches the tippy edge of his tongue and makes him pull back just a little. These things never happen in movies, do they?

They probably don't even happen in real life except to klutzes like me.

"Let's go sit on the pier," he whispers and starts to move me off the dance floor. But I stop him and tell him we only just got here and it'd be fun to dance a little longer.

"We'll come back later." Now he's sounding very insistent and I'm beginning to feel very confused. The first thing that comes to my mind I really don't like but there it is. Looks to me like he's in a mighty big hurry to get out there on the pier again, and I know it's not just to talk. That thought gives me a funny feeling. I'm not really sure what it is but I know it's not so good.

He smiles and gives me a sexy little wink and says, "Come on, I won't bite you." And it's very tempting, but something happens inside my head and I just don't move. He looks surprised and I guess I am too.

We're standing there in the middle of the dance floor and he's saying come on, and I'm saying I don't really want to right now, and this goes back and forth and finally he walks off the floor. I don't want to just stand there, so I follow him to the bar where everybody is standing three deep. I feel bad and very embarrassed, very depressed, like I could cry any minute.

But I don't. I just stand there next to him and we both pretend we're watching the dancers.

He's still next to me so maybe it's not so bad. I turn to look at him, but he pretends he doesn't see me and just stares straight ahead.

Maybe he really does want to talk. Maybe I insulted him by not even just going with him to rap for a while. No wonder he's angry. It was really babyish of me to think that all he wants to do is make out with me. How are we ever going to have a relationship if I don't trust him? That's it.

"Listen, Jim," I say, "I'm really sorry I acted that way. If you want to go . . ." And right in the middle of my apology he takes off. He just walks away. I watch him and I can't believe my eyes. I run after him and grab his arm. "What's the matter?" I ask, my voice trembling. "Can't you even tell me what's wrong?"

He shakes my arm away and stares hard at me. "Come back in a year or two," he says. "You have a lot of growing up to do." And he turns away and goes up to another girl, a pretty blonde, and pretty soon they're dancing.

My throat chokes up and tears fill my eyes. I'm in the middle of a crowded disco but now I don't see anything or anyone. I can't just stand here with tears running down my face. I've got to get out of here but I can't even see enough to find my way out. Naturally I don't have a tissue so I have to wipe my eyes with my sleeve so anybody watching me must know I'm crying. Who cares? As soon as I can see in front of me I push through to the door. I hear Anita calling me but I don't even turn around. I just keep walking until I start running and I'm really crying.

I hate him! I hate him with all my heart. How could he do that to me! Finally I'm crying so hard I have to sit down on a bench on the side of the walkway, and I just sob like I haven't done since I was really little. I've never been so unhappy in all my life.

And there's something else. I've been a terrible person. I'm really surprised at myself. I'm not at all like I thought I was going to be. I would hate it if someone else acted the way I did—to Barry and even Gloria, I mean.

I can't believe how bad I feel.

I get back into the house and thank goodness everybody's sleeping, so I just go up to my room and get into bed and turn out the light. I wish I was home. I hate it here.

15

Tuesday morning is crazy because Cynthia has to make an eight o'clock ferry to be in the city for an eleven o'clock appointment. She overslept so we all end up flying around the house trying to help. The rushing pays off because she just barely makes the ferry. Actually they hold it a couple of seconds for her. The kids are jumping up and down, shouting, "Wait! Wait!" while Cynthia races down the dock. One of the men gives her a hand and she leaps on. We stand there waving until she's far out of sight.

I hope she doesn't run into my parents. I told you we live in the same apartment house, and it could be embarrassing since I never spoke to Cynthia about the sleeping-out business. I'm going to but I'm just waiting for the right moment. She probably won't see them anyway because she said she was only stopping off there to pick up something and then going right on to her appointment.

In all the furious activity I didn't have any chance to think about yesterday. Ever since I got up this morning I've had a sort of heavy feeling, and now that everything's quieted down and I start thinking about how horrendous yesterday was I almost feel sick. I practically wish I'd never come out here. Maybe I can't really make it on my own. All I know is that I keep doing things that make me feel terrible the next day. There must be something awfully wrong with me if that keeps happening.

In all the rushing to get Cynthia on her way, the kids never did eat breakfast, so I fix the usual when we get home. They're just finishing when somebody knocks on the front door. We don't even have a bell and the door is always unlocked (almost always). That's one of the special things I like about Fire Island, you never even think about being scared. It's really open and very safe.

DeeDee jumps up from the table and runs to open the door. I hear a happy squeal and I can't figure out who's there so I poke my head into the living room and get a big shock. It's an old man, with lots of white hair, dressed in a suit and tie. He has DeeDee in his arms, and, right away, the first thing I think is, Damn it, it's Mr. Landry, and I want to sit down and cry because everything is just so awful and now this.

"Is this Victoria?" Mr. Landry asks DeeDee, and she nods and says to me, "This is my grandpa," and gives him a big squeeze with all her might, and he laughs and gives her a big kiss on the cheek.

All this time David was upstairs changing into his bathing suit, but when he hears who's here he comes charging down the stairs two steps at a time and practically jumps into his grandfather's arms, which happen to be completely filled with DeeDee.

"Hold it! Hold it!" Mr. Landry says, and with a lot of laughing and hugging he struggles free. You can see he loves it.

"Grandpa! Victoria said you couldn't come," David cries. "She said you had to go to the doctor with your friend." David sounds like he's practically accusing me of something.

"Is that what she said?" Mr. Landry acts surprised. The rat. I can't believe he's going to stick me with a bum story. "I guess she just wanted to surprise you," he says. I know the kids love him but I don't think I'm so crazy about him.

"I didn't tell anyone about the phone call,

Grandpa," says DeeDee, "and Victoria says I'm going
to get the button."

"The button?" he asks.

Naturally he doesn't know anything about the special grandpa club button. Still, you'd think he'd play
along. But all he says is, "Never heard of it." He's
really beginning to bug me.

"Where's your mother?" he asks, looking around
like he didn't know she was going into the city. The
kids tell him where she went.

"Looks like I missed her," he says, "but I'll catch
her when she comes home." Then to me, "When's she
coming home?"

"Dinnertime, I guess," I say.

"Shame," he says, "but I gotta leave around five. It's
okay, though, I'll catch her the next time."

Damn. He sneaks out here when he knows Cynthia's
away, spends the day with the kids, and then disappears and sticks me with explaining to their mom.

The kids keep bugging him to eat something, and
finally he says okay, he'll have some coffee. All the
while he keeps asking what train Cynthia is making
and trying to figure out what ferry she'd be making if
she was going to get home for dinner. I think he's kind
of nervous about being here.

After his coffee he plays with the kids and he's
really terrific with them. He makes them laugh with
some crazy imitations of a barnyard and what happens
when Cornelius's cat gets into the chicken coop. And it
really is funny. Even I laugh.

What isn't funny is how he jumps when Steven from
across the street comes in. Then I realize that he's
afraid about Cynthia. I don't know how come I didn't
see it before, but he's so crazy about the kids that he
takes a chance and comes all the way out here just
because he has to see them and all the while he's really
scared about meeting Cynthia. It takes a lot of guts to
go someplace where you're not wanted and you could

even be thrown out. Cynthia would do that. She's that angry about her ex, Jed.

Anyway, it's terrible to see a grandfather have to sneak around just to see his own grandchildren who love him. And it's not as though he's a bad man. At least I hope he isn't. I mean, think about it, suppose you get an old man who's a criminal. He's probably someone's grandfather. Anyway, anyone can see Mr. Landry isn't a criminal.

The big excitement is when he tells them that he's going to rent a little dinghy and they're all going fishing. They positively freak out and it takes us ten minutes to calm them down. I get DeeDee into her bathing suit and they get their towels and life preservers and they're ready. Mr. Landry says he's going to buy some sandwiches and they'll have a picnic on the boat.

I figure that since he's on Social Security he probably doesn't have all that money, so I say, "Why don't I make the sandwiches here?" and for the first time he looks a little grateful. I suppose maybe he thinks I'm on Cynthia's side and he doesn't trust me too much. I'm not so crazy for him as a person, but as a grandfather he's terrific.

Mr. Landry doesn't want to change at the house so he stops into the pizza bar and puts on his fishing clothes and packs his regular clothes in a brown shopping bag. He ends up looking like one of those old New England fishermen. He's even got the hat with the flies stuck on it.

Anyway, I walk them down to the dock, where he rents a little sailing dinghy because all the fishing dinghies are already out. People go fishing really early. The boat's a perfect size for the three of them.

They go off, and I realize that the kids haven't argued once since their grandfather came. He must be magic because mostly they can't be together for two seconds without fighting. Just like Nina and me.

Nothing to do but go home. Just as I get to the

house the phone is ringing. I make a run for it. Maybe it's Jim. Maybe he reconsidered. Even if I did act a little immature last night, still, that's the kind of thing people can talk over and straighten out. I grab the phone on the fifth ring. At least I don't have to worry that it's Mr. Landry.

"Hello," I say. Let it be Jim.

"Victoria? It's me, Anita."

"Hi, what's up?"

"That's what I was going to ask you. How come you weren't at the beach this morning?"

"Yeah, well . . . DeeDee had a sort of stomachache so we hung around here. She's okay now."

"Good 'cause we were wondering if something was wrong. You left so fast last night. I mean, I called you but you just kept going." I know she's fishing for the story of what happened with Jim, but she's not going to get anything from me. She's okay, Dana is, too, but they're not my good friends. I only just met them, so I don't expect them to stand up for me or anything like that. But I don't like the idea of them gossiping about me either.

"Gee, I'm sorry," I say, "I didn't hear you calling me. I had to rush because I forgot that I promised Cynthia I'd be home by nine-thirty. There was something urgent she had to do and she needed my help."

"Well, we thought something was wrong because you left alone." She's dying for the real story but she's never going to hear it from me.

"Yeah, I know, Jim was really upset but I told him to stay and dance. I think I'm getting a little tired of him anyway."

"Yeah?"

"Sort of . . . what's up, anyway?"

"Nothing much. I was just wondering if you're going to be free tonight."

"I don't know. Why?"

"Dear old Ron just called from the city and he's got

some business thing so he's staying over, and lover boy is out of town so Eva is stuck home. I thought maybe I'd go down to The Monkey tonight. Wanna go?"

"I don't know yet. Cynthia's in town, too, and I don't know what time she's coming back."

"Sounds cozy."

"What do you mean?"

"You know, Ron and Cynthia both in town together."

"Yeah, sure." She's really beginning to bug me, so I tell her I have some things I have to do and that I'll call her later, and hang up.

Well, I have a whole day to sit around and be miserable about yesterday. I probably sound like it's not so bad, but really it's horrendous. I can't see how I can face any of those people again in my whole life. It's even terrible what I did to Gloria. She never did anything to me except be Jim's girl friend, which isn't something you can exactly blame her for. And Barry. How can I be so awful to hurt him again after what I did the first time! And Jim? He's not a whole lot better than I am. We make a great pair except that I don't really think we're ever going to be a pair again. I think he's going to go right back to Gloria, and I bet she'll take him back. When it comes to Jim, she's really got it as bad as me.

I sound like I have it all figured out, but I absolutely don't except for maybe one thing. I think I'm still so hooked on Jim that I would do almost anything to get him back, and if it means trying to act more mature, I guess I would do that too. That's all I've been thinking about since last night.

I actually sit on my bed most of the afternoon and even cry a little because I feel so unhappy. I probably should have gone to camp like I did last year and then I wouldn't have all this trouble. In camp you can be a little kid again. They do all the thinking for you. I'm beginning to think this being on your own, like now, is for the birds. Not really, but it is tough to be able to do practically anything you want. There's just too many ways to make mistakes.

I would call my parents but I couldn't tell any of this to my mother. She'd probably be shocked and maybe she'd tell my father and then I'd really die. I could send a letter to Steffi, but she's away with her father on a camping trip, and anyway I don't think I want to put everything down in a letter. It'd be too depressing. I didn't commit a crime or anything like that, but you know what? I feel like I'm in one of those old movies where this rat of a girl, the trampy siren, steals the heroine's boyfriend (not that I see Gloria exactly as a heroine) and the rat steps all over everyone and you really hate her and that's just what I feel like.

I can hardly believe that's me because I always see *myself* as the heroine. In my fantasies the Glorias are bad and I'm terrific. In my dreams *I'm* the one who gets the boy because I'm so wonderful and good. But this time I got him because I'm really bad. Except maybe I didn't exactly get him anyway. I'm confused.

I don't even feel like lunch, and when the phone rings I practically jump out of my skin. It's got to be Jim. I pick it up and say a really little "Hello."

"Victoria? It's Cynthia."

Oh, oh.

"Everything okay? The kids okay?"

"Everything's great. Were you on time for your appointment?" Oh, God, I hope she doesn't ask to talk to the kids.

"Right on time," she says. "Thanks for your help."

"I almost freaked out when the boat started to move out." Maybe I can keep her mind off them.

"Me too, but I made it. Listen, honey, I've run into a little problem and I need your help."

My help? First thing I think of it's more shrimp.
"Sure," I say. What can you say when someone asks
your help.

"I may have to spend the night in the city because
there's a late appointment I should keep."

Oh, no! I'm torn. I promised my parents that I
wouldn't stay alone overnight with the kids, but it
would work out so great if she didn't come home tonight. Mr. Landry could spend the day with David
and DeeDee and then he could go home and I could
invent some Big Secret Day or something and they'd
keep quiet about their grandpa and then maybe that
would be the end of it. I mean, he would have seen the
kids and that would keep them happy for a while, and
then there wouldn't have to be any horrendous scenes
when Cynthia came home. Maybe Cynthia could
straighten things out with Jed and nobody would have
to know what happened until everything was okay
again. And anyway, it would only be this one time
that she would sleep out, and my folks wouldn't ever
have to know. I know it's the wrong way to do things,
but I'd go nuts if I had to face any more problems
right now.

"It's okay with me, Cynthia," I tell her. "Don't
worry, I can handle things here."

She gives me a few instructions—who to call if I
need any help and how to lock the front door. I can
tell she's absolutely delighted about the arrangements
and is so hot to get off the phone that she doesn't even
ask anything else about the kids. Except by now I've
got it together and I could tell her how David and
DeeDee are across at Steven's. It's awful how if you lie
once it seems you have to keep on lying. You always
have to cover it with another one. I'm never going to
get myself in a hole like this again. Boy, will I be glad
when this day is over.

I wonder if Anita is right. About Ron and Cynthia

having an affair, I mean. It fits right in with the rest of this mess.

I get back to thinking about last night and make myself even more miserable about Jim. It can't just end this way. I have to see him once more. And I don't care how. I decide I'm going to call him as soon as he gets off work about five. Then I think about how badly it's all been going and how gross I acted and finally I guess I just cry myself to sleep.

16

The next thing I know, someone is shaking me awake. I open my eyes and squint and it's Cynthia, and for a minute I don't know whether it's morning or night. I can't figure out what she's doing waking me up, and then I remember about Mr. Landry and the kids and I nearly panic.

"Victoria," she says, standing over me. "What's going on here!" I can see she's angry. "Where are the children?"

"The kids?" I sit up. I search around frantically for something to tell her and then see it's not nighttime. "How come you're home so early?" Now I'm really confused.

"You're damn right I'm home early," she says, and she's not just angry, she's furious. "Why didn't you tell me your parents didn't want you to stay alone overnight? I asked you if it would be all right. Why didn't you tell me?" And she charges on without even letting me get a word in. "What a damn embarrassment to run into your mother in a crowded elevator and have her inform me that I cannot leave you alone here at night." Cynthia continues. "Why did you lie to me?" Oh, no! They *did* bump into each other. Just my luck.

"I'm sorry . . . I didn't mean . . ." I start to apologize but she cuts me off.

"Where are the kids? Are they at Steven's?"

"What time is it?" I've got to get myself together.

"What difference does that make? Where are they? Tell me this instant!" Now she's in a panic.

"It's okay, Cynthia, they're okay. They're with their grandfather." You can't fool around when someone thinks their kids are missing.

"What do you mean they're with their grandfather? Where? What's going on here?"

"He came to visit them . . . and . . ."

"Their grandfather came out here and what—he's with them here, or took them away? *Tell* me." She looks like she's going to explode.

"Well, he didn't actually take them." That sounds like he stole them or something.

"He's got them, hasn't he?"

"Well, yes, but . . ."

"You let him take my children! How dare you decide such a thing when I told you I didn't even want him to talk to them on the phone!" She comes toward me like she is going to attack me and I move back.

"Where are you going?" she demands.

"No place. I'm really sorry . . ." I never in my whole life had anyone outside my family yell at me like this and be so angry. I know I'm going to cry any second.

"How dare you disobey me with my own children! Who do you think you are!" Now she's practically screaming at me and I'm too scared to cry. Please, God, let her calm down.

Just like on command she stops and says in a quiet mean voice that practically spits at me, "Where are they now?"

"Fishing." I manage to get it out in a very small voice.

"At six o'clock!" Again she's screaming. "Are you telling me they're out on the water at this hour?"

"I don't know . . . they're probably on their way back."

"They damn well better be." She spins around and

says, "Come with me." And she pounds down the stairs.

I don't even stop for my shoes. I just race after her. That was rotten of Mr. Landry to keep them out so late. Why did he have to do that? I knew I didn't like that man. Boy, he doesn't care about anyone but himself. And after I was so nice to him. He really stinks. I can hardly see the stairs because now that she's stopped yelling at me I'm crying.

Cynthia doesn't even stop at the door, she just pushes through and lets it slam in my face. I follow her but I manage to stay behind her. I'm afraid she'll start screaming at me in the street. She is steaming mad. We get to the dock and I don't see the kids or Mr. Landry anyplace around. We look for the woman who rents the fishing boats, but there's nobody on the pier.

"Well"—Cynthia turns to me—"now, where did they go?" As if I would know.

"Maybe he took them for something to eat or something . . . ice cream! That's it. He must have stopped in . . . with them."

It has to be because they never let anyone pass that store without buying them a cone. I run on ahead to the ice cream store but I can see they're not there. Barry is alone behind the counter. My heart sinks.

"Barry?" I pull open the screen door and poke my head in. "Did you see David and DeeDee?"

He's surprised to see me. "Who?"

"You know, the kids I take care of."

"Oh, yeah . . . no, I didn't see them."

"They were with their grandfather. They must have come in here."

"I've been here since eleven this morning and they haven't come in."

"Oh . . ." and I can't help myself. I start to cry again right in front of Barry.

"Hey, what happened? Are they missing or something?"

"They were with their grandfather. . . ."

"Hey, come on, nothing to cry about. If they were with their grandfather"—and he comes out from behind the counter—"they're fine. I bet he took them for something to eat."

By now Cynthia is here. "Well," she says, "where are they?"

"Barry says maybe Mr. Landry took them for something to eat," I say.

"Yeah," Barry says, sticking up for me.

"Have you seen them?" Cynthia asks Barry, and he says no, and then her whole expression changes and she looks scared instead of angry. Then she says, "Maybe they never got back. Maybe they're still out there and something's happened." And without another word she shoves the screen door open and races out and toward the pier. Barry and I run after her.

There's still nobody on the pier. It looks as though all the sailing dinghies are in, but there are so many you really can't tell. Still, the woman wouldn't have gone home if one of her boats was still out.

"They must be back because the woman wouldn't have gone home with one of her boats still out, right?" I say to Barry more than to Cynthia. I'm sort of afraid to talk to her.

"That's right," he agrees. "She wouldn't leave until all the boats were in." But Cynthia looks like she's not about to trust either of us.

"Who owns the boat rental?" Cynthia asks Barry.

"Mrs. Randolph and her son Charlie," he says. "They live across there over the grocery store." He points to an old wooden two-story house. Before he even finishes showing her, Cynthia starts running across the street.

"I'll just die if anything happens to them," I say to

Barry. "It's all my fault." I'm feeling almost sick to my stomach.

"What do you mean?" he says. "I thought they were with their grandfather."

"They were, but they weren't supposed to be. It's a long story, but Cynthia doesn't want them to see their grandfather."

"Is he a bad guy or something?" Of course Barry is confused.

"No, nothing like that. It has to do with her ex-husband. He owes her money so she said his father can't see the kids—oh, it's all a big mess."

"She sounds nuts not to let the kids see their own grandfather."

"I know, but that's the way she wants it, so I guess I should have listened to her. After all, they're her kids. Oh, I don't know. I wish I'd never come out here. . . ."

"Hey, come on, they'll turn up." He's really a very nice guy, which makes me feel even worse because I was so awful to him.

"Hey, look," he says, pointing out on the water. "There's a small sailboat coming toward shore." It has to be them. Please, let it be them. We both run to the end of the pier. As the boat comes in closer, we can see that there's only one person in it. Even closer I can tell it's only Mrs. Randolph alone. She pulls the boat up to the pier and Barry runs over to grab her line.

"Mrs. Randolph," Barry shouts to her, "did the man with the two little kids come in yet?"

"They sure didn't," she answers, and my heart falls three feet. "That's who I was looking for." And she climbs up on the dock and ties up the second line. "They're almost two hours late and I was getting worried. They got whitecaps out there now, you know."

This is becoming a nightmare. Cynthia comes running up to us out of breath, saying she can't find the woman, and we tell her this is Mrs. Randolph, and then she finds out that the children and their grandfather are still out there. Mrs. Randolph leaves out the part about the choppy water, but Cynthia's face turns white anyway, and she grabs my shoulder as if she's going to faint. Mrs. Randolph says she thinks they'd better alert the police and the Coast Guard, and then she tries to calm Cynthia by saying they probably ran aground around the cove. Lots of people do, and there's no danger because they can walk to shore from there. That helps Cynthia a little but she's still frantic. Mrs. Randolph takes Cynthia back to her house to call the Coast Guard, and Barry tells me to wait here while he locks up the store and gets his speedboat, and he runs off.

I wait alone at the end of the pier and start thinking how all this is my fault. Then I start thinking about David and DeeDee. If anything ever happened to them . . . but I can't even finish the thought because it's so horrendous. I'm glad I at least made them wear life jackets, and then I remember that Mr. Landry didn't have one and I think, gee, he's pretty old and if the water is rough . . .

In the middle of all this I start thinking about how angry and disappointed my parents are going to be about the business of me staying alone with the kids. They may even make me come right home. It probably won't make any difference—coming home, I mean—because Cynthia's certainly going to fire me anyway.

I'm so involved in thinking about all this mess that I don't even see Barry pull up in his speedboat.

"Hey, Victoria! Over here," Barry shouts from the boat, and when I turn around, my stomach does another drop, which brings it about to China. Jim is with him. Right now he's the last person in the world I want to see.

Barry puts out his hand and I grab it and jump in. I try to give Jim a casual "hi" but only half of it comes out words and the rest gulp. He's busy throwing lines and pushing the boat away from the dock and the other boats, and Barry is steering and I kind of creep into a corner and hope nobody notices me.

Mrs. Randolph is right, the water is awfully choppy and we're bounding up and down, banging hard every time we hit the water. Naturally I pick the worst seat, and every time we hit the water a cold spray smacks me in the face, taking my breath away. Barry turns around and waves me up with them. Hanging on to the rails for dear life, I creep up to where Barry and Jim are and squeeze between the two front seats. At least there's a plastic shield that keeps off most of the spray. Barry shouts something to me, but the noise of the motor and the splashing is so loud I can't make out what he's saying.

I finally understand that he wants me to let go of the wheel. I can always count on me to do the dumb thing. Barry is breaking his neck trying to steer the boat in all this mess, and I have the wheel in a dead man's grip. I let the wheel go and grab onto Barry's arm which also makes steering impossible except I have to hold something. Jim pokes me and points to a metal bar right in front of me that I can hang on to.

It becomes even rougher as we get farther from shore, and all I can think of is those little kids and how scared they must be and poor Mr. Landry—how awful he must feel because he really loves them so much.

Still hanging on to the metal bar, I let myself slide down to the floor with my back against the instrument panel. This way I end up facing Barry and Jim. They're both standing there. Barry is steering and Jim is squinting into the wind, searching the water. The wind is whipping their hair back and they're both wearing sweat shirts, the kind with the hood except the hood won't stay up.

Boy, Barry is a nice guy. I didn't even have to ask him anything. As soon as he saw something was wrong he jumped in to help. I mean, he didn't have to go out searching himself, but I guess that's the way he is.

I suppose it's pretty nice of Jim, too. Except I don't think of Jim as nice like Barry, which sounds peculiar. But I don't mean it as a criticism of Jim, it's just that now that I know them both a little better, I think Barry may be a nicer guy. I still dig Jim much more.

"They didn't say anything, just that they were going to try for flounder," I tell Barry.

"That means middle fishing," he says to Jim, and he heads the boat out toward the center of the bay.

It's so rough now that it feels like we're in the middle of a squall.

"Hey, buddy," Jim shouts to Barry, "this could be really dumb."

"What do you mean?"

"Going out in all this," Jim says. "It's getting too rough for this size boat. We should head back."

"We can't!" I say first to Jim, then again to Barry, and I'm practically pleading. "We have to find them. Don't you realize they're just two little kids and Mr. Landry, and he must be at least—I don't know—almost seventy. And I don't even think he has a life jacket."

"Hey," Jim shouts to me above the wind, "I know it's serious, but I'm just saying we can't handle it."

"We have to," I say, mostly to Barry.

"No, we don't," Jim tells me, "that's what they've got the Coast Guard for. They know what they're doing. They have equipment, the power boats and helicopters and everything. We don't belong in this thing. All we're going to do is get ourselves in trouble."

Suddenly he got to be forty years old. I can't believe he's acting so awful.

"You could be right," Barry says, "but I'm willing to take the chance. I figure it's safe enough to take a couple of fast swings around the area."

Hurray for Barry!

"They're probably holed up along shore someplace and we're risking out lives for nothing." Now Jim sounds almost nasty, but it's two against one so there's nothing he can do about it. For the first time since I've know Jim I feel angry at him. Even what he did last night didn't make me feel this way.

Barry steers the boat in big circles, trying to cover as much of the bay as he can. No luck. The sea keeps getting choppier and now it's starting to rain. It really is a squall.

"Look," Jim says, "I told you you're not going to find them. Come on, buddy, let's head back. This is crazy."

"Please, Barry." I practically beg him. "Just a little longer."

"It's getting very hard to handle the wheel," he says, and I can see it is because every time we hit a wave both of them have to hang on to the wheel for dear life. "Maybe we should head back."

"Smart boy," Jim says, pleased that he won.

Gross. How could he be pleased that he won such a horrible kind of argument!

"How come," I say to Jim, "if the Coast Guard is so great, we haven't seen any of their boats, and no helicopters or anything else?"

"Believe me, they're out here," he says, "looking in the right places. They do these kinds of searches twenty times a week."

"Maybe," I say, "but if we haven't seen them yet, they're not looking around here, and if the kids are here they're not going to find them. Barry?" I turn to him. "Can't we just look around this part once more?"

"Okay, we'll head for that tower over there," he says, pointing to a lighthouse on the mainland, "and then we'll circle back around that cove. Okay, Jim?"

"What am I supposed to say? It's your boat," he says, and he looks really annoyed.

Barry heads the boat across the bay toward the

tower, and we all keep looking all around, trying to spot the kids and the old man. It's getting harder and harder to see because the rain is coming down heavy now and the sky is black.

I see a piece of wood in the water and my heart stops. Maybe it's part of their boat, and I point it out to Barry (absolutely not to Jim) and he says no, it's only a log.

"I told you we're not going to find them," Jim says to me. "We're only one little boat on this whole great big bay. No way we can find them if they're even out here. They're probably back on shore and we're risking our necks for nothing. God, what a dumb idea."

All the while he's talking to me I'm busy searching the water. I don't even look at him. I may not ever look at him again in my entire life.

"Come on," Barry tells him, "it was worth a try. The more people looking the better the chances of finding them."

"Baloney. They're back at the dock," Jim says, and I pray like crazy that this time he's right.

A bolt of lightning cuts through the rain and I jump six inches off the floor. I'm terrified of lightning on the water. I'm about to ask Barry what would ground the lightning on this boat, but I'm afraid he'll say "us," so I just swallow the question. I always knew I should have listened in that damn science class.

Just as we're making the last turn I think I spot something.

"Wait! Wait!" I'm shouting and pointing over the side. "Over there!" But over there keeps changing because the boat is rolling so much. Whatever I saw is gone.

Barry circles the area I was pointing to, but there's nothing there. The rain is coming down in sheets now, and Barry turns the boat lights on—not that it helps us see, but at least other boats can see us.

We search blindly for another ten or fifteen minutes

and don't see a thing. I've never felt so bad in my whole life.

"Hey, look!" Barry suddenly shouts, pointing to something off the right side of the boat. "There *is* something there!"

It takes all three of us to turn the boat and keep it heading into the wind. Whatever's in front of us now isn't very far away, but the going is so rough we can only inch along. A couple of times we lose sight of the thing, but Barry keeps the boat straight on 40 south on the compass. We're practically on top of it before we see it again.

It's the boat with the kids and Mr. Landry!

I don't even bother saying, "I told you so," to Jim. I'm so relieved to see them, even Mr. Landry, that tears well up in my eyes and I practically begin bawling out loud.

The kids are huddled together in front of the mast in the cockpit, in water almost up to their waists. Mr. Landry is at the tiller trying to steer but doing nothing but spinning in circles. The sail is torn and flying in all directions. That must have been why they got lost. A sailboat's useless without a sail.

The kids go crazy when they see us. They start jumping up and down and waving, and we shout to them to sit down, but they can't hear us over the motor and the storm. We motion wildly for them to sit. Mr. Landry gets the idea and with one hand still on the tiller leans way over and pulls them down.

Barry motions for Jim to take the wheel and tells him to head off the bow of the other boat. He's going to make a grab for their mast.

Mr. Landry sees what we're trying to do. He moves to the mast and wraps one arm around it and holds out the other to Barry.

Jim swings the boat around twice, but both times it's too wide and they miss each other. I hold on to Barry's leg so he can lean out farther.

Again Jim makes a pass at the little boat, and this time Barry grabs Mr. Landry's hand. But a wave hits our boat and it breaks their grip. When the wave hits the dinghy it catches Mr. Landry off balance, and we all watch in horror as he slips off the narrow deck and into the water on the opposite side of their boat.

I can hear the kids screaming and I start to scream myself. Barry grabs one of the lines and dives off after Mr. Landry. The kids are hysterical and hanging over the side. I know they're going to fall in any second.

"Head into their boat," I shout to Jim, "and I'll try to jump in."

"Take the line with you!" he calls to me as I crawl along the side of the boat up to the bow.

I take a line and wrap it around my waist. I don't even know why or how it'll help, but it seems like a good idea. I turn back to Jim and he's nodding his head yes. It must be right.

We head in toward the dinghy and I set myself to leap. I have no sneakers. It's slippery. I don't have a life preserver and I'm scared to death. But I have to get to those kids because if I don't do it fast they're going to be in the water.

Our boat's coming in closer. I can't wait too long to jump because one big wave can take us past their boat in a second and then we'll have to make an entire turn, which could be too late.

The little dinghy is still pretty far away but I'm so afraid of another wave that I let it come only a tiny bit closer and make my leap.

It's got to be the biggest jump I ever made in my life. I feel like I'm flying, and then I hit their deck and slide right into the mast. I made it!

In two seconds I'm in the cockpit and I've got both kids down with me and I undo the line around my waist and wrap it fast around the mainsail cleat. There's a jerk and we go flying after the bigger boat. We're attached.

Meanwhile, Barry's got the line around Mr. Landry and he's hanging on to the side of our boat.

"I'm going to bring him over to my boat," he shouts up at us. "You'll tip if we try to get in."

And with his arm under Mr. Landry's chest, he gets him over to the speedboat. Mr. Landry looks so limp it's scary, but I tell the kids everything's okay, he's going to be fine.

Barry and Jim manage to get Mr. Landry into the boat, and he collapses into a heap in the cockpit. Jim doesn't lose any time getting us out of there, and even though it takes us almost an hour to get back to the pier and we're sitting in waist-high water we're dumb enough to feel that we've made it. In fact we're all smiling. Even Jim.

Wouldn't you know it, just as we're getting in, the rain stops and it's practically calm by the time we reach the pier. It probably looks like the whole thing was a snap.

The pier is jammed with people. Practically all of Ocean Beach is down at the docks. Cynthia is right in front and she's crying and laughing, and when we hand the kids up she nearly devours them with hugs and kisses. David will be complaining about that for the next month.

Even Mr. Landry isn't in as bad shape as I thought. They have to help him onto the pier and he looks weak and exhausted, but he can stand on his own two feet. Not so steady, but he's standing.

I dread the moment when Cynthia calms down and sees me and Mr. Landry. I can tell Mr. Landry dreads it too. Everybody is jumping around and making a big fuss, and even the Coast Guard is there. They're using walkie-talkies and calling in all their boats, and it turns out they even had helicopters out looking for us. And everybody wants to know what happened and everyone's talking at once so nobody knows what actually happened, but we're all happy and smiling and exhilarated.

Barry and I try to help Mr. Landry because he really is wobbly. The kids see us and run to him. "Grandpa! Grandpa!" they both shout and start pulling him by the hand and hugging him.

Cynthia just stands there looking at him. God! This is going to be horrendous.

The kids keep pulling at Mr. Landry, and he keeps shaking his head no and urging them to go along with their mother and saying he'll catch up later.

All the time Cynthia just keeps staring at him. I can't believe she's going to be so mean to that poor old man.

"Henry," she finally says, and you can't tell from her tone if it's good or bad.

"Hello, Cynthia," Mr. Landry says, and you can see he's really embarrassed and very uncomfortable. He mumbles something about how it turned out to be quite a mess and how he's really sorry for it, but the kids cut him off, shouting how he's the best sailor in the whole world.

"Oh, Mommy," David says, "you should see how Grandpa steered the boat even with those big waves and he wasn't afraid of anything. Right, Grandpa?"

"Well, David," Mr. Landry says, "now that it's over I gotta admit it was a little hairy there for a while, but you and your sister were so brave I knew we'd make it."

"We were scared when you fell off, Grandpa," DeeDee says, hugging his legs. "I was crying, and you were too, David."

"You fell overboard?" Cynthia asks, horrified.

"I was not crying," David says, sounding like his old self.

"You were too," DeeDee says.

"Well," he says, "that's only because it was Grandpa

and I thought he was going to drown and that's why."

Cynthia stands there with her mouth open while Barry tells her the story of how Mr. Landry climbed up on top of the boat and hung off trying to reach him and how he'd slipped. Barry leaves out the whole part about how he saved Mr. Landry's life.

But Mr. Landry puts that right and shakes Barry's hand and thanks him and then hugs him and everybody smiles and it's hero time and you should see Barry's face. Is it red!

Cynthia keeps watching Mr. Landry, and there he is with the kids hanging off him, dripping wet and looking sort of frail and really old, and finally she comes over to him and puts her arm around his shoulders and says, softly, "I'm glad you're safe."

"Thanks," Mr. Landry says, smiling, and all the time his eyes are full of tears. "I'm very sorry, Cynthia . . . and you, too"—and he looks at me very apologetically, except he can't remember my name—"uh . . . mother's helper . . . very sorry for what I did. . . ."

"Forget it, Henry," Cynthia says before I can say anything. "I was a fool to tell you to stay away from your own grandchildren. I don't know what I thought I was accomplishing." Then she stands back and looks at him. "What a mess! We have to get you into some dry clothes."

"Oh, that's okay," he says. "As soon as I get back to the city . . ."

"Are you kidding? You're not going back to the city like that."

"Sure I am, it's not so bad. A little damp here and there."

"Henry," she says, "I'm not going to hear another word. You're coming back to the house with us, and we're going to round up some clothes for you, and you're going to take a good rest—for about a week."

"A week!" DeeDee exclaims. "Whee!"

"Hey, that's neat," says David. "We can do lots more fishing."

"Well, Cynthia," Mr. Landry says, and you can see he's so close to tears he can hardly talk, "if . . . you're sure. . . ."

"I am absolutely sure, Henry, absolutely." And she gives him a hug and a big smack-type kiss on the cheek. The kids are jumping up and down, out of their heads with joy. Mr. Landry is all smiles.

Me too. I couldn't bear the thought of anything else bad happening to that old man.

"I think we all deserve a little celebration," Jim pipes up. "How about it? A drink for the heroes." And then he looks at me. "And for the heroine."

"Hooray for the heroine!" Barry shouts, and now my face gets all red.

Barry asks everyone to be quiet, and then he tells how I jumped across to the dinghy to get to the kids before they fell in and he makes it sound like Wonder Woman at work. When he finishes everyone says, "Hooray!" and I think I'm going to die of embarrassment.

I don't believe this whole scene, but I have to admit it feels great.

"Thank you," Cynthia says to me, "for what you did . . . for all of us." And she looks like she's going to cry, and I feel like I am too.

"I'm really sorry, Cynthia," I say. "You were right to be angry with me. If I didn't go against you, none of this would have happened."

"Maybe not," she says, "but the more I think about it the more I feel the mistake was mine. I made a bad decision and expected you to carry it out. It wasn't fair to you, to the kids . . . to anyone."

"All along I felt bad about doing it behind your back," I say to her. "I'm sorry about that."

"Well, when you think about it," she says, "blindly following a bad decision is a lot worse." Cynthia looks really pleased with me and I feel terrific.

It's turning out to be a sensational day and I feel very proud. I hope it doesn't show too much in my face.

"You *should* feel proud," Cynthia says, smiling at me.

There goes my see-through face again.

"How about it?" Jim says. "Should we head for The Monkey?"

"Not me," Barry answers. "I just want to get home and get these wet clothes off. If you want to come with me"—and he looks mainly at me—"I can offer you some iced tea."

"I'll pass on the iced tea, thanks anyway," Jim says, and then turns to me. "How about it? You want to hit The Monkey for a while?"

He's asking *me*. Jim actually wants *me* to come with him. All my plotting and planning, all that's happened, finally pays off. I can't believe it.

"Thanks," I tell him, actually both of them, "but I think I should go home with the kids. After what they've been through today I think I should stick with them."

"Sure thing," Barry says. "You have a raincheck for any time you want."

"Thanks," I tell him, "and thanks for helping me. Both of you. It would have been a disaster if you both hadn't been super." But I'm looking directly at Barry as I say it.

Then Cynthia thanks them both and Mr. Landry thanks them again and Cynthia thanks me again and this could go on forever except, thank goodness, Dee-Dee starts jumping around a lot saying she has to make pee-pee and everyone laughs and we all start back.

All five of us tramp into the house, all wet and sandy, and the phone is ringing. David picks it up.

"It's your mommy," he says and hands it to me.

This is going to be rough.

17

I'm out in rough water swimming as hard as I can to reach a buoy that keeps moving and bobbing away from me. I'm just about to grab it when something small and soft slides into my hand and pulls at it. I think it's a fish and try to get my hand away, but the little something holds tighter and tighter. I jump up and, of course, I'm in my bed and the little fish is DeeDee, who stands there at the side of my bed, holding my hand and grinning her cute smile with the missing teeth.

"Oh, God, DeeDee, not yet," I moan, covering my face with the pillow. I feel her creeping under the covers, and I know sleep is hopeless. She's like a jumping bean in bed.

"Where are the hands?" I ask her the same question every morning.

"The big hand is on the twelve and so's the little one."

"Can't be," I tell her.

"How come?"

"Because then it would be twelve o'clock."

"Oh."

"Go look again, okay?" And she runs down the steps while I hide back under the covers. Something about the day feels strange. DeeDee comes back all out of breath.

"Now, little cookie, where is the big hand?"

"On the one."

"That sounds right, now what about the little hand?"

"It's stuck on the twelve."

Crazy! I bend over the side of my bed and look out the window. It does look different and it's noisier, and I think DeeDee's right. It's twelve. I can't believe it. The little monsters let me sleep till noon.

I jump out of bed, almost knocking my head on the ceiling. I'll never learn.

"What happened?" I ask DeeDee. "Where is everyone?"

"Everybody's sleeping except me and you. Was your mommy mad at you last night?"

Oh, she must have heard me on the phone with my mother.

"Well, she was a tiny bit angry at first," I answer. More like out of her head furious, but I don't tell Dee-Dee that. For a full five minutes my mother did a nonstop number on how my not staying alone overnight had been the most important condition of the job and how could I completely disregard their rules? Obviously I was too young for such a responsible job. Then she went into how I probably shouldn't be out there all by myself and was working herself up to how maybe Cynthia ought to look for someone else, and somewhere in there she had to stop for breath, and that's what I was waiting for.

I started talking and told the story right from the beginning. When I came to the part about Mr. Landry visiting the kids and how they were almost lost in the storm, she was stunned. Then Cynthia got on and told her how I jumped in the boat and saved the kids. I love to hear the story even though it changes every time someone else tells it. Naturally it gets better.

My mother was very impressed, and then we had to wait while she recounted it all to my father, and then I got back on the phone and they asked me a million questions about the rescue and everything.

In the end they understood. My father agreed that there were extenuating circumstances and mostly I had made good choices and they were very proud of the way I handled myself in an emergency.

"But please, Victoria," my mother ended up saying, "next time you get in over your head, remember we love you and care about you, and all you have to do is call us and we'll help you."

So it ended up that they were pleased and proud of me, and when your parents feel that way about you nothing can be too wrong with the world.

"Anyway, DeeDee," I say, and give her a kiss on her tiny nose, "they're going to come out and visit us this Sunday."

She loves that idea and when I tell her they're going to bring her a surprise she can't wait.

"Can we go to the beach today?" she asks, folding up my pj's until they're practically small enough to put in my wallet and then stuffing them under my pillow. She's a terrific help.

"Sure thing. Right after we eat."

"Is he going to come?"

"Who?"

"The boy in the living room."

"What boy in the living room?"

"The one from yesterday," she says.

Can't be. But it has to be. DeeDee doesn't play tricks like that. "Why," I ask, "didn't you say something before?" I guess I sound sort of aggravated because she screws up her face as though she's going to cry and says, "You didn't ask me."

"You're right. I forgot." And I give her a hug.

"I love you, Victoria," she says and gives me a big wet kiss on my cheek.

"I love you, too," I say and hug her again. I think she's getting to be less of a monster. I hope.

When the love scene finishes, I ask her which boy is in the living room.

"The big one," she answeres. No help. To her, both Jim and Barry are big. But I know it has to be Barry because Jim wouldn't come here. That's not like him to just pop in. He's sort of a big-shot type, and I know he'd expect me to meet him somewhere or better yet come over to where he was. It must be Barry. Great. Maybe he'll come to the beach with us. He'd probably be wonderful with the kids. Then I let my mind dance around a little. What if it's Jim? I guess that's like all the dreams I had coming true—and on my terms too. What a thought!

I send DeeDee downstairs to tell whoever it is I'll be there in a second, and then I race down to the second floor bathroom and brush my teeth, wash up, and comb my hair the best I can. Nice, if you like rat tails.

I take my time walking down the bottom flight of steps. Can you imagine if it really was Jim? That would be like saying he was very interested in me. What a fantastic summer this could be! The three of us could hang out together. Jim, me, and Barry. You know, I really like Barry a whole lot now that I've gotten to know him better. I probably *like* him even more than I like Jim. But that's not the point. My feelings for Jim are completely different.

I hear DeeDee regaling whoever it is with a wonderful tale of how my mother was angry with me last night but now she's not and did he know that when she, DeeDee, wakes me up in the morning sometimes I curse?

I move a little faster. God knows what else she'll decide to tell him.

No question about it. I want Jim Freeman to be standing in that living room. My luck, it'll be Steven.

But it isn't. It's Jim. Super!

"Hi," I say, smiling like crazy.

"Hey." He smiles back. "You snuck up on me. I was listening to some very interesting stories."

"Oh, God, DeeDee, don't you dare." And I pretend to be horrified. I know I told you he was very hand-

some, but I think he got even better looking overnight. The sun has put white streaks in his straight
blond hair and turned his skin this absolutely fantastic
apricot color. He's positively gorgeous. The kind of
person people turn around and stare at.

"Come on, DeeDee." He picks her up in the air and
she squeals in delight. "You and I have a few things to
talk about."

"No, you don't," I laugh. "DeeDee, don't you tell
him a thing."

"Oh, yes," he says, and we play this back and forth,
and Dee Dee loves it, but I can see she's trying like
crazy to come up with something, so I cool it because
she really could produce a few beauts.

I take DeeDee into the kitchen and set her up with
a tuna sandwich, and when I come back into the living
room Jim is sprawled out on the couch looking
through the sports section of the *Times*. So far he
hasn't said why he came by. As soon as he sees me he
puts the paper down and says, "So what do you want
to do today?"

Like a dummy I answer, "I don't know . . . I have
the kids, you know." I guess with Jim the terms have
to be his.

"Are you stuck with them all day?"

It's a funny thing, but I haven't been feeling my
usual uptight heart-racing kind of thing with him today. In fact, something's bothering me but I don't
know what it is.

"If you put it that way, I guess so."

"That's okay. Why don't we all go down to the
beach this afternoon? I know where I can get a kite. I
bet the kids would love that."

"Are you kidding? They'd freak out. They love
kites."

"Terrific. I'll get the kite and meet you down at the
bay beach in about three-quarters of an hour."

"No good," I tell him, "the kids hate the bay beach."

"Well, just tell them that's the only place I can fly the kite." And he starts to open the screen door. "See you at one-thirty."

And he's out the door.

"Wait! Wait up!" I run to the door and shout.

He stops and turns to me. "What's up?" he says.

"It won't work. DeeDee's terrified of the bugs and things on the bay beach. She absolutely won't go."

"Then you want to forget the whole thing?" Suddenly he's angry. And I know he's talking about a lot more than the kite and the beach. And then it hits me what's been bothering me about him since yesterday, maybe even before that but I guess I didn't know it. I think he may be a little spoiled.

Actually, a lot spoiled. Spoiled rotten, I think that's what they call it. I told you how he was so fantastic looking, really gorgeous, and that he has a very charming personality—you know, charisma and all that. So naturally with that combination people are always fighting to be with him and catering to him, and by now he's come to expect it all the time. He's the guy in charge of all the hanger-on-ers, and it bugs him if someone doesn't do things his way. Like now about the beach or even yesterday when we were searching for the kids. As soon as he saw he wasn't in charge he didn't really want to be part of it, and it has nothing to do with his being afraid of the storm. He is definitely not a coward. It's worse.

He's arrogant. We bruised his ego, Barry and I did, just because we didn't let him run the whole show. The fact that we were trying to actually save people's lives, little kids'—that was secondary. The big thing to Jim Freeman was who's running things, and if it wasn't going to be him—well, then, forget it, and that went for the kids too.

I don't know how he and Barry could be such good friends. I mean, they're so different. Like yesterday. Barry didn't give a thought about his boat or himself or anything. All that mattered was finding those kids.

Funny how I guess I never looked much deeper than Jim's good looks. I suppose I'm pretty much like everybody else that way, but now, knowing what kind of person he really is, I'm beginning to think that maybe he isn't so gorgeous after all and that I don't want to go to the beach with him today—or any day.

He's still standing there, good old arrogant Jim, waiting for my answer, and you can tell by looking at that confident face that he expects me to crumple up and practically beg him to let me go with him to the bay beach.

"Okay," I tell him, "then let's just forget the whole thing."

Beautiful. For a half second even his suntan turns ashen, but Jim Freeman types recover fast.

He shrugs a kind of "your loss" shrug and turns and starts walking down the street.

Watching him walk away, I have a sinking feeling in my stomach, and I almost want to call him back but I don't. Am I making a mistake? God, I hope not. I let this great thing walk out of my life when I could absolutely have him (nobody's going to believe it, anyway) and I don't do a thing. This just isn't me.

Or is it?

Because it feels right.

I walk back into the house and sit down on the bottom step and try to decide whether or not to cry. After all, it's not every day you fall out of love for the first time. It's not such a bad experience. Disastrous, but not really too bad. So I decide not to cry.

And I make another decision.

I go right to the phone and I'm just about to dial when I see this note propped up against a little vase on the table. I open it. It's from Cynthia. I didn't even know she wasn't home. It's another one of her cuties. It asks me "pretty please" will I give the kids and Mr. Landry lunch and put in a load of laundry and then there's a shopping list for when I get back from the beach and could I be a "positive pussycat" and iron her white pants outfit. If the "best little shrimp cleaner in the country" wants to clean the shrimp in the refrigerator she has no objections. The note ends saying I'm a doll and she's over at the Walkers' for the afternoon. It's signed, "Love ya to pieces, Your Summer Mother."

It takes me about ten seconds to decide what I'm going to do. I grab the pen next to the phone, turn Cynthia's note over, and *the new me* writes:

> Dear Summer Mother,
>   Could you pretty please hem my pink skirt and my black pants and I'm missing four snaps on my white blouse, two buttons on my jacket, and the zipper on my red shorts is stuck. Could you do them before the weekend? I would be forever grateful if you could spare an itsy-bitsy 45 minutes every evening to help me with my logarithms for extra summer credit. Love ya!
>
> Your Summer Daughter,
> Victoria

Now I dial, and as I listen to the phone ringing at the other end I begin to feel very happy about a lot of things and more excited than I expected about making this phone call.

Yes, going to the beach with *someone* today is definitely a terrific idea, but Jim just happens to be the wrong person.

"Hello," the right person's voice says.

"Hi, Barry, you dried out yet?"